Upshots
and Other Stories

London Short Story Prize 2015 Anthology

Published by Kingston University Press London

Spread the Word is London's literature development agency, celebrating, supporting and advocating for the diversity of London's writers and connecting them with readers. As well as offering workshops, masterclasses, 1-2-1s for emerging writers, our flagship projects include: Writing the Future; research into the diversity of fiction publishing in the UK; Young Poet Laureate for London and Flight 1000; a paid year-long apprenticeship and training programme for people from backgrounds underrepresented in the publishing industry.

spreadtheword.org.uk
facebook.com/spreadthewordwriters
@stwevents

Kingston University Press publishes high-quality commercial and academic titles and works with partner organisations to bring projects to life. The KUP list reflects the diverse nature of the student and academic bodies at Kingston University in ways which are designed to impact on debate, to hear new voices, to generate mutual understanding and to complement the values to which the University is committed.

@KU_Press

Published by Kingston University Press and Spread the Word

fass.kingston.ac.uk/kup

spreadtheword.org.uk

A catalogue record of this book is available from the British Library

First published in 2016
The moral rights of the editors and authors have been asserted

UPSHOTS
ISBN-13: 978-1-909362-06-2

Contents

Acknowledgements

Huge thanks to:

The writers whose stories make this anthology; Joanna Campbell, James Woolf, Gary Budden, Jean Ashbury, Stephanie Scott, Damien Knightley, Tyler Keevil, Nikesh Shukla, Frances Gapper and Sabo Kpade.

Judges Jon McGregor, Kevin Barry, Elise Dillsworth, for their warmth, generosity, diligence and creativity.

First readers Zoe Ranson, Isha Karki, Jarred McGinnis, Irenosen Okojie and Paul Sherreard. Paul McVeigh and Mark Banting and all at Waterstones Piccadilly, for a great London Short Story Festival 2015; the start of this year's prize journey.

Short story writers Kerry Barner and Hana Riaz.

All at Kingston University Press, especially Judith Watts.

Lucy Beale, for managing the London Short Story Prize so diligently. Ruby Cowling, for your kindness and brilliant foreword.

And finally, to all Spread the Word's supporters and all who read this anthology.

Thank you.

Foreword

I am delighted to write this foreword for Spread the Word. It was a huge privilege to be awarded the London Short Story Prize in 2014, and the publication in 2015 of Flamingo Land and Other Stories was the genuine highlight of my writing year. Spread the Word have been endlessly supportive: they manage to make you feel as if you're the only writer in the world, that their entire reason for existing is to champion you. Considering how far from reality that is, that's a heck of a skill.

I find the short story form a constant source of joy and surprise, and (to my taste, at least) it is best when it's allowed to roam free. The free-range short story is not confined by the battery cage of the common 2,000-word limit, nor is it forced to run longer than a few sentences if it doesn't need to. It is happier when not enslaved by rules we might encounter such as "never have more than one point-of-view character". The richness of these ten stories results from the writers' willingness to give their stories the space to be what they are – be that quiet and contemplative, or sparky and full of twists – and their confidence in the risks they take with language and subject matter.

In keeping with the almost completely open pasture given to form and length, this competition specified no theme – and these stories are as varied in scope, setting and subject as much as tone. But while reading, I kept returning to a sense that each one is built around something either we, or the main character, does not want to know. A little black hole at the heart. A moment of shock, or a rising dread, or a sudden wrong-footing. For all that, there is much humour here, too. But when short stories are good, like these, they're discomfiting as well as entertaining, and perhaps it's down to that feeling: we're being pulled by the hand toward something we don't want to know.

But on to the important part: the ten stories that form this book.

James Woolf was Highly Commended in this year's Prize for R v Sieger – additional documents disclosed by the Crown Prosecution Service. Woolf sidesteps the traditional narrator, instead leaving it to the reader to piece together the story via scant emails, phone transcripts, and the reports of various professionals who get dragged in as matters escalate. Here, the main character is the one resisting things she doesn't want to know, caught between her own burning neurosis (the source of which becomes horribly clear during one phone call) and the inconvenient necessity of staying polite – brittly, Britishly polite – with people who will insist on standing in one's way. The very funny, very unfortunate situation that emerges is all the funnier and more unfortunate because Woolf hasn't told it straight.

Joanna Campbell won the London Short Story Prize 2015 with the beguiling, expertly crafted Upshots. Thanks to the idiosyncratic charm of the young narrator, Stan (whose 'brain-cogs are cock-eyed') and Campbell's skillful use of the small detail to draw the big picture, we know straight away we're in good hands, so we don't need to be orientated straight away. We don't need telling where we are or what's about to happen. Instead we relax and wait for the story to unfold – a story of complicated morals in a 'broken', 'rusting' post-war Yorkshire, and the innocent compulsion to put right a mistake. Upshots pleases the ear and warms the heart, even while it drags us toward a conclusion we're pretty sure we really don't want to know. Judge Kevin Barry referred to its 'delicious blend of light and shade', and indeed, it's a delicious, immersive and unpredictable experience.

If you look at Saltmarsh from a distance, you'll realise that in terms of action the narrator simply walks to the pub to meet a friend. However, Gary Budden's rich, sensitive language and subtly apt observations mean that this walk – along a seven-mile stretch of the Swale from Faversham to Whitstable in Kent – becomes an intense reading experience in which any further events are unnecessary. Narrator Simon's soulful responses to the natural world are set against his nostalgia for a youth more interested in the pleasures of the built environment, and while he is not overtly in crisis, he is struggling to fully situate himself in either the city or the countryside. A curlew cries 'like bubbles from a mouth submerged' and we are left with our own questions of how (or whether) we can find our own 'elsewhere at home'.

When the short story addresses enormous and complex events such as those which attended the 1947 Partition of India, we might think it'd be like trying to capture the Atlantic in a wine glass. But when it's as deft and needle-sharp as Stephanie Scott's Partitions, it can illuminate a momentous historical upheaval with lasting emotional impact. Hindu teenager Lakshmi and her best friend Joshna, a Muslim, are wrenched apart when the country is split along sectarian lines and Lakshmi is forced to flee – disguised by a headscarf the girls have embroidered between them. Lakshmi may or may not survive the journey into the Punjab mountains: our anxiety for her is left in the air at the story's close. Scott cleverly lets us see only a glimpse of the violence Lakshmi is fleeing, and in the same way that the very smallness of the short story can make it an effective frame for large narratives, her restraint forces us to acknowledge the thing we don't want to know.

Ten-year-old Yasmin, the would-be 'warrior princess' of Lemonade With Ice by Jean Ashbury, is a refugee whose post-traumatic symptoms manifest as seizures, particularly on Bonfire Night when her body reacts to the evocative auditory assault of fireworks. Sadness permeates this story, but, crucially, it's our sadness; it arises naturally thanks to the authentic semi-innocence of Yasmin's voice, and Ashbury's light touch in showing us the world Yasmin and her family have fled and the one in which she finds herself now. Like the schoolteacher who shuts down Yasmin's attempts to draw the horror she's come from, we don't want to know about what war does to children, so a direct description can't trigger this emotional response. Instead, sadness comes through Yasmin's longing for the simple loveliness she's lost: a family, together, drinking home-made lemonade 'in the garden by a wooden table under a big white umbrella'.

In Chibok, Sabo Kpade takes us directly and unapologetically to the Nigerian town from which 219 schoolgirls were abducted by Boko Haram (sometimes translated as "Education is Forbidden") in April 2014. In a voice that continuously moves in and out of emotional territory – as if in shock – Kpade draws out the story of one of the abducted girls who has managed to escape. Her abduction and capture are told matter-of-factly; the story's focus is on her return and of the complex response of other missing girls' parents. Should they see her return as a sign of hope, or hopelessness? Apart from her physical injuries, from which some of the adults shy away, she is changed in ways that begin to set her apart from the community. She has witnessed her friend Paulina make different and (to us) unimaginable choices in an impossible situation; she has seen what she might have become. Believing 'everybody deserves to be free whether they be young girls, rams or a wooden stool if it is able to breathe', she lets the rams out of their pen, and even though the animals return voluntarily 'because they don't know any other home' – and even though 'being free is an empty feeling' – she retains her belief in freedom as a principle. Finally, she cements a further belief: that, in spite of the risk and the opposition of the men in her family, the offer of a university education is worth grabbing with both hands.

The 'quasi-mythical' Greek island of Sikinos is the setting for Tyler Keevil's *Cassandra to the Sea*. Appropriately located right in the middle of the Aegean, it has become home for the last months of a dying, 'drying-up, landlocked' woman whose life and career have been tied up with the sea. Her big-hearted, clumsy brother, narrating the story, is the one she wants with her at the end: it will fall to him to take her into the water as she dies and weighs her body down under the waves. But he doesn't want to know: he doesn't want to accept what Sandy has accepted long ago, and perhaps as a result there is a kind of parapraxis in the tragi-comedy of errors that he sets in train. Actually, their awful journey is not at all comic, either for him or for us; thanks to Keevil's masterful timing and stark description, the brother's low point is quietly devastating. Cassandra is the one who can still see the funny side. It's her response to all this which carries the emotional heart of the story: 'It had to be you,' she says. She's chosen to entrust her death to her brother precisely because he is who he is, with all his faults, and in the end the beautiful realisation comes – like a bubble rising through the water – that this story was about love and redemption all along.

Before we return to the UK we visit Lamu, an 'island operated by donkeys' off the Kenyan coast, for the appealingly relatable story *A Man, Without a Donkey* by Nikesh Shukla. Narrator Raks has come to Mombasa to scatter the ashes of his cousin Naman, and now he's on Lamu for the weekend to deliver Naman's bequest to the island's donkey sanctuary. Raks feels compelled to honour his 'not pivotal' cousin – to make him matter. Looking at Naman's life has made him uncomfortable: perhaps he, Raks, has fought a bit too hard for his independence, relies a bit too much on his WiFi ('solitude never means being alone anymore. It just means being by yourself'), and has become islanded. So he's happy to meet seemingly-carefree Ingrid: accompany for the next few hours at least. However, sooner than expected, Raks has to face his own solitude once again, to 'face [his] burdens alone'. Shukla's achievement is to make Raks instantly likeable, and in doing so make us feel his aloneness all the more keenly.

Lucy Ludicrous can 'mould light', and admits to using this magic for occasional mischief in Frances Gapper's *The Moustache Maker's Daughter*. Though Lucy's language is fanciful and archaic, her phrases 'merry-alive', the setting is explicitly contemporary, so we wonder if there's something real she's avoiding: something, perhaps, she doesn't want to know. And, in fact, it's the loss of her mother that comes daily to her consciousness: 'as usual' she glances up at the roof (her mother fell off 'while gathering moss for our Organic Adventures

Foreword

range of moustaches') and when a moustache slips due to the cheap glue they provide customers, she curses not her penny-pinching father but the 'absent parent'. In 'jest' she dons a moustache herself and dresses as her young father, hoping to seduce both 'blonde Susie' and the handsome, freshly-mustachioed 'Chevron', the way her father seduced her mother. (It's a delight to see this romantic freehandedness go unpunished in the narrative, to see Lucy spared of all neurosis in relation to her love objects.) Gapper, like her character, 'moulds light': using the lightness of a teasing, mischievous narrative to gesture toward the repercussions of loss. In spite of its tinge of grief, the story stays on the sweet side of bittersweet.

The Colorado River Toad and the Racoon by Damien Knightley rounds off the anthology. It's a tale of love that is 'almost real' – with everything that implies. Whenever he refers to his 'divine mystery', Emilia Rose Parker, we can tell the narrator has savoured that voluptuous name a thousand times on his tongue. He is helplessly buried under her 'love yous', her 'we have forever' mantra; his heart is an 'over-inflated balloon'. Compared with her perfection, he is a worthless toad – and happy to accept it. Frustrated, but optimistic, he knows his chess-playing lover will always 'outdo' him, but everything's okay because 'it won't be long before she materialises'. And indeed, she does finally take a kind of form. Of course, that thing he didn't want to know was what he knew all along. (Didn't he?) This is The Frog Princess turned inside out, and told in an utterly modern way.

Each of these stories rewards repeat readings – for me, doing so has been a pleasure and an education. Congratulations go to all ten authors, to the competition judges and to Spread the Word for curating this book.

Ruby Cowling, February 2016

London Short Story Prize Winner 2014

Preface
The story behind the stories

At Spread the Word, London's writer development agency, we love finding new writing that excites and challenges us. Sustaining relationships with writers, working with them to ensure their craft is honed and their careers are progressing in a way that's right for them is what we are all about. This is the main aim of our annual London Short Story Prize, to champion the short story form by finding a wide range of original new stories for readers.

Our London Short Story Prize 2015 was the Prize's third outing, (originally the 'Spread the Word' prize in 2013), and we were lucky enough to work with talented and generous judges, award-winning writers Jon McGregor, Kevin Barry and London agent Elise Dillsworth, to help us identify the top stories that make up this anthology.

In 2015, we opened the competition up nationally, whereas in previous years we focused on London writers. Additionally, we joined the 21st century and went 'green', calling for submissions using online platform Submittable, and introduced an entry fee for the first time. We're really pleased to have partnered with the wonderful folks at Kingston University Press to produce this anthology.

The criteria was purposefully flexible – all we stipulated was that stories submitted were 8,000 words or less. The idea behind this was to ensure that any talented short story writer felt welcome to enter. We would like to thank the 400 writers who entertained and moved us with their short story submissions.

The stories in Upshots are written by many different types of writers. For some, this is the start of their writing journey, and for others, this anthology will sit in a list of prestigious publications. We recognise that competitions are important to writers' careers; they can validate and bring talent to the attention of a wider audience. The power of being listed is incredibly useful for writers' experience, career progression and confidence.

I'll let the words of the judges tease you into two of the ten stories.

On Joanna Campbell's winning story Upshots:

Jon McGregor:

> "Upshots was a real treat to read. There's a confident use of voice and perspective which pulls the reader through the story with tremendous energy. The disjunction between the way the

narrator sees the world and the way the reader understands the world to be is well-handled and subtle; and is then put to good use in a lovely sleight of hand towards the end. Technically accomplished, and a very worthy winner."

Kevin Barry:

"Here is a story that proceeds line by line on the sheer intensity of its linguistic invention. Very quickly, inside a couple of pages, its sentences succeed in building a world. The language is an uncannily successful blend of a rhythmic dialect and a tightly controlled prose that combine to bring this world alive on the page. The dialogue sings, and the action is expertly depicted – the plot, meanwhile, keeps us thoroughly unsure of our footing, and takes us in unexpected directions. There is a delicious blend of light and shade in this story, and I don't think there's a single wrong note in it."

Elise Dillsworth:

"Engagingly told story of a family bound by secrets and how an action done with the best of intentions narrowly misses the worst of outcomes. A heart-stopping moment of revelation in a story that is nicely paced and coloured with humour and sharp insights. The writing manages to convey depth without overstatement and the rich use of language and sense of place makes for a deeply evocative and rewarding read."

The judges on James Woolf's highly commended R v Sieger - additional documents disclosed by the Crown Prosecution Service:

Jon McGregor:

"It's always a treat to come across a story where the form has been led by the content, and this story - consisting of emails, letters, telephone transcripts and other documents - has utilised the device very successfully. I particularly liked the moments of indirect and partial revelation, and the increasingly rich pictures of the supporting characters which built up as the story progressed. An excellent use of technique."

Kevin Barry:

"At first glance, this is a story that suggests tricksiness, with its scattershot collection of documents, reports, lists, texts, mails. But very quickly we become aware that we're in the hands of a real storyteller, and the narrative is expertly shaded in and teased through. I thought this story was genuinely funny – in a way that induced large, stomach-heaving honks of laughter – but beneath the humour there was a freight of real sadness, or even darkness, and it was this that elevated the work above its own constraints. I thought the timing, especially, was fabulous."

Elise Dillsworth:

"An original, fresh and deftly handled story where the intrigue intensifies as details are subtly revealed to the reader. The writing shows a great confidence of style and, along with an acute eye for witty observation, made for a very satisfying read."

It's been a pleasure working with the ten writers included in this anthology, and I'm certain you'll enjoy reading each and every story. Please take a moment to read the writers' biographies, follow them on Twitter and show them some appreciation if you can.

Laura Kenwright, January 2016

Spread the Word

Notes

The Spread the Word Prize in 2013 was won by Clare Fisher and judged by Bidisha, Courttia Newland and Tania Hershman. Edgeways and Other Stories – published in December 2013, available on ebook.

The London Short Story Prize 2014 was won by Ruby Cowling and judged by Jackie Kay and Cathy Galvin. Flamingo Land and Other Stories – published in November 2015, available on ebook and hard copy ISBN 9780954008352

The London Short Story Prize 2015 was won by Joanna Campbell, and James Woolf was highly commended. Judged by Jon McGregor, Kevin Barry and Elise Dillsworth.

James Woolf

Author of R v Sieger – additional documents disclosed by the Crown Prosecution Service

Highly commended in the London Short Story Prize 2015.

James began writing short stories two years ago. In that time, the form has become something of an obsession. R v Sieger – additional documents disclosed by the Crown Prosecution Service was longlisted in the Fish short story competition and the Short Fiction prize before being highly commended in the London Short Story Prize. Connectivity was commended in the Segora international short story competition.

Prior to this, James' plays have been produced in various off-West End venues including The King's Head Theatre, the Arcola and the Theatre Royal Margate. In addition, two of his radio plays have been broadcast, including Kerton's Story with Bill Nighy, Lesley Sharp and Stephen Moore on Radio 4. He has also written adverts (including about 10 for Black and Decker), and worked for two years as a writer in residence in a prison.

He is married with two daughters.

Twitter: @WoolfJames
Website: woolf.biz

R v Sieger – additional documents disclosed by the Crown Prosecution Service

Mathison Mayhew Solicitors
0203-242-0082
enquiries@m-m.co.uk

Dear Helen

As you know, the Crown Prosecution Service (CPS) has to release all documents and other material it intends to use for a trial in advance. This is the latest batch that we have received. Very happy as ever to discuss or answer any questions.

Freya

Freya McCarthy-Jones
Partner

1

R. v. Sieger – additional docs disclosd by CPS for trial bundle.

Beasley Catholic High School, 11 Somerset Road, New Barnet, EN5 1GP

Ms Helen Sieger
Derry Towers
Monken Hadley
Barnet
Hertfordshire
13.12.2013

Dear Helen

Further to our meeting earlier today, we write to confirm our joint decision that you will be withdrawing Jonty from Beasley Catholic High School with immediate effect. As a gesture of good will, we will refund your fees to the value of the final three weeks of the Autumn term. I believe that we are in agreement that the local media need not become involved in this matter. You may expect to receive a cheque from our Bursar in the next few days.

I would like to take this opportunity to wish Jonty all the very best for his musical endeavours and future education.

Yours sincerely

Heather Spencer

Mrs Heather Spencer
Head Teacher

from:	Helen Sieger <Helen.Sieger99@gmail.com>
to:	Fiona Crossley <FRCrossokay@Yahoo.co.uk>
date:	19 January 2014 14:29
subject:	The saga comes to an end

Hi Fiona

Finally, finally –there's light at the end of the tunnel. After the fiasco of Beastly High (about which you could go on Mastermind!) we had a meeting at Archbishop Alderwood's. Poor old Jonty a little nervous – I told him, "What happened was NOT your fault. There can only be so many bullies and unreasonable people in the world. (We just happen to be meeting most of them!)."

They were actually INCREDIBLY accommodating. Jonts preparing to start next week! They totally got the music thing –how couldn't they after hearing him sing 3 arias in the staff room (which has a C Bechstein piano by the way! - the music teacher promised to have it tuned soon). Just had lovely letter from the head, I quote: "We are so looking forward to Jonty joining us and taking full advantage of his considerable musical talents!" Was SO tempted to send copy to Heather Spencer!

btw, have you heard anything from my darling ex-husband? Not that I care if I never see him again, but difficult for Jonty.

Listen babes, catch up soon? I'll line up a child minder and we'll paint Barnet red!

Bestest

Helenxxx

Singing from the Heart

NEW YEAR NEW START

Apologies for lack of recent postings. So much going on!

The big news is that I've quit National Youth Choirs of GB! We won't say too much, let's settle for "artistic differences". You'd have thought that they would welcome the odd suggestion for the summer programme (DUH! - it's called enthusiasm!)

I'd only been singing with them half of my life by the way.

I'm now very much on the prowl for other opportunities. Anyone need a talented eleven year old SOPRANO?

On a similar NOTE, have just started at Archbishop Alderwood's School. My mum specially wanted me to say a big thankyou to Head Teacher, Mr Lyons, who's been incredibly supportive – even dropping into lessons to check I'm settling in. Sweet! He's also the first Head I've met to appreciate why I simply CANNOT play contact/team sports. (Advice from our insurers btw - they involve shouting so present big pinkie risk to my VOCAL CORDS!).

And finally, please stop by my website to catch up on my latest recordings. I am sure you'll love listening to Bach's *Jauchzet Gott in allen landen.*

Also, Dad – if you're reading this, have you got a new number? I'd love to hear from you (you old toe-rag).

Jonty

EXTRACT FROM SCHOOL REPORT: 03.04.14

SCHOOL REPORT CARD

Student: Jonty Sieger

Year 7

Music

Teacher: Iain Anderson

Jonty possesses the voice of an angel and has superb understanding of music theory. Considering his gifts, he is extremely modest and an absolute pleasure to have around.

Although he's been with us only a few weeks, I can safely say it's a privilege to teach Jonty. I am sure that many musical opportunities will present themselves for Jonty at Archbishop Alderwood's, not least next term.

from: Archbishop Alderwood's School
to: ALL PARENTS
date: 3 April 2014 11:12
subject: IMPORTANT MESSAGE FROM MR LYONS

Replies to this email are not monitored

Dear Parents,

I am delighted to announce that following the intensive building programme on the western perimeter of the school, the Duchess of Cambridge will be visiting Archbishop Alderwood's to open our brand new gymnasium next term. Further details about this highly prestigious event, including how pupils will become involved, will follow shortly.

Please find attached:

- Newsletter - please note the dates on page 3 for the forthcoming term.
- Sports Day 2014 - from our PE department: response from Parents required.

May I take this opportunity to wish you all an enjoyable Easter. We return on Tuesday 22nd April.

Kind regards

Robert Lyons
Head Teacher

1	won't ever be going there again, bloody imbeciles! How these
2	people ever expect to run a successful restaurant is beyond
3	me!
4	HELEN SIEGER: Are you recording this?
5	SALLY HINES: Of course.
6	HELEN SIEGER: Why?
7	SALLY HINES: You know why --
8	HELEN SIEGER: It's not [inaudible] --
9	SALLY HINES: We've been through this a million times --
10	HELEN SIEGER: Not respectful to me, mum --
11	SALLY HINES: I'm not [inaudible] right now. What were
12	you phoning about?
13	HELEN SIEGER: Kate Middleton is visiting the school.
14	Opening a gym or something --
15	SALLY HINES: Kate who?
16	HELEN SIEGER: The Duchess of Cambridge.
17	SALLY HINES: Lovely.
18	HELEN SIEGER: I'm going to get Jonty to sing for her.
19	SALLY HINES: Make sure I get a decent seat this time.
20	HELEN SIEGER: We're [inaudible] in any case. D'you think
21	it's the right thing to do?
22	SALLY HINES: What?
23	HELEN SIEGER: Arrange it with the school?
24	SALLY HINES: Of course, why not?
25	HELEN SIEGER: The Beasley woman said I was too
26	demanding. I do wonder sometimes.
27	SALLY HINES: Oh not that idiot! Aled Jones did a private
28	recital for Princess Diana, didn't he?
29	HELEN SIEGER: Probably.
30	SALLY HINES: And Pope Paul. And the Queen I think.

31	HELEN SIEGER: Really?
32	SALLY HINES: So it's not exactly "demanding" to request an
33	audience with the Duchess of Kent--
34	HELEN SIEGER: Cambridge --
35	SALLY HINES: Whatever.
36	HELEN SIEGER: The school's said the pupils will be doing
37	something special. And the music teacher dropped a whopping
38	hint about next term. I'm half expecting the Head to call me.
39	SALLY HINES: And he sang at Bob Geldoff's wedding. The
40	year you nearly --
41	HELEN SIEGER: We've moved on from Aled Jones, mum.
42	I'm trying to talk about Jonty.
43	SALLY HINES: I expect he's rehearsing before school --
45	HELEN SIEGER: He does three hours every evening.
46	SALLY HINES: Not enough. That was your downfall --
47	HELEN SIEGER: I have to accompany [inaudible]gets tired
48	at school --
49	SALLY HINES: If you'd practised like --
50	HELEN SIEGER: Not Young Musician of the Year! --
51	SALLY HINES: Yes! You'd have --
52	HELEN SIEGER: Can we talk about Jonty? --
53	SALLY HINES: I can't believe Brind won it.
54	HELEN SIEGER: Still going on about 1986!
55	SALLY HINES: You were so much more talented.
56	HELEN SIEGER: And you said that to his mother. Look, I've
57	got to be --
58	SALLY HINES: Always rushing off –
59	HELEN SIEGER: I have to collect him –
60	SALLY HINES: Leaving me to pick up the pieces.
61	HELEN SIEGER: What pieces?
62	SALLY HINES: It doesn't matter – really it doesn't.
63	HELEN SIEGER: We'll speak soon.
64	SALLY HINES: Whatever, Helen – [inaudible].
65	THE TELEPHONE CALL FINISHES.

Local boy to sing for Duchess

By Matt Dobson

A BARNET boy aged 11 is to give a personal singing recital for the Duchess of Cambridge when she visits his school next month. Jonty Sieger will perform a selection of his favourite arias, many of which can be purchased through his own website.

Jonty's mother, Helen Sieger, is a concert pianist and professional keyboard and singing tutor. She began voice coaching with Jonty when he was just 2 years old. By the age of 7 he'd already passed all 8 grades of his singing exams, most of these with distinction.

Jonty told us that for the last fortnight, he has been up at 5.30am every morning practising, in readiness for the royal visit to Alderwood's School.

"I just can't wait to perform for Kate as she is someone I've always admired," said Jonty. "My dream is to become a virtuoso when I'm older." With performances like this under his belt, he already seems well on his way to making that dream become a reality!

It is four fourteen in the morning and my head is spinning, have tried meditation and mindfulness (my mind is too full for mindfulness). Just need to get it out of my head and onto paper - Fiona says she does this when she gets stressed. It's starting to unravel and I'm beginning to think this school is the same as all the others. I thought it was a formality. I didn't bother troubling Mr Lyons directly, why does he need to be involved with the minor details I thought. So I telephoned Beverly his secretary and mentioned that we'd need the Bechstein moved to the gym (for the big event). So after I'd spelt Bechstein and explained that it's actually the piano in the staffroom she said could you remind me which event your talking about (bit of an airhead!). Jonty singing for the Duchess of Cambridge, we'll need a piano, he couldn't do this a capella, I replied, not unreasonably, before telling her it's two words and spelt a capella. The secretary said it sounded "super" and that she'd come back to me but was "sure it wouldn't be a problem". She did come back to me (the same day to be fair) and said actually it was "a bit of a problem", the Bechstein being rather heavy and not possible to move to the new gym (apparently at opposite ends of the school). "Not a problem at all" I said – please tell Mr Lyons I'm on good terms with a company that will deliver a 1936 Steinway model O to the gym and collect it the very sane evening. She sounded a bit surprised by this and asked whether that was a model O as in the letter O and then said she would speak to Mr Lyons tomorrow. I suggested she might want a word with him now as this was somewhat important but she explained she had childcare responsibilities. Next morning she called to say Mr Lyons wanted to thank me for thinking of the school but didn't consider it necessary for me to go to the trouble and expense of hiring a Steinway piano. It's really no trouble I said, and as to the expense he needn't worry as my ex-husband was in banking and Fiona Shackleton earned every penny of her fee when it came to the divorce settlement. The secretary said she'd rather got the impression that Mr Lyons hadn't known anything about Jonty singing for the Duchess of Cambridge. He'd said something about this being a short visit with no opportunities for passing entertainment. I explained as patiently as I could that she'd be more than happy to hear anyone of the calibre of Jonty singing, and that a story in the local press had already led to interest from the BBC in an item for the Breakfast Show (which would be fabulous publicity for the school). Beverly's shorthand was clearly failing her at this point as she asked me to confirm the spelling of Shackleton so I suggested that Mr Lyons might want to cut out the middleman and call me on my mobile. That was 37 hours ago and I still haven't heard from him.

from:	Helen Sieger <Helen.Sieger99@gmail.com>
to:	Robert Lyons <rlyons@ArchbishopAlderwood.barnet.sch.uk>
date:	6 May 2014 08:02
subject:	Performance at Bishop Alderwood's

Dear Robert

I do hope you had a restful bank holiday. I thought it might be useful for me to send a brief email explaining my thinking about Jonty singing at Bishop Alderwood's on 19th May. I fear that there may have been some crossed wires last week as everything was going through your secretary (who was, I have to say, most helpful and polite). I got the impression from Beverly that you might have preferred a fuller dialogue about these plans at an earlier stage and if that's the case I must apologise. My intention in phoning the school was to consult over the arrangements rather than to present you with any kind of fait accompli.

Perhaps it would help if I explained the sort of programme I had in mind. I was thinking that even though we are talking about the Duchess of Cambridge, the tone should be uplifting rather than overly formal, so I would suggest the following arias:

- Ave Maria – Charles Gounod
- Because – Guy d'Hardelot
- O Promise Me – Reginald De Koven
- The Lord's Prayer – Melotte
- L'Amero Saro Costante – Mozart

The Mozart works best with a string quartet – but I wouldn't wish to complicate things at this stage.

As I think I said to your secretary, I can provide the piano and do all the accompaniment myself, so you'd just need to arrange a seat for Kate. Or a throne perhaps!

Best regards

Helen

12

from: Helen Sieger <Helen.Sieger99@gmail.com>
to: Robert Lyons <rlyons@ArchbishopAlderwood.barnet.sch.uk>
date: 7 May 2014 11:13
subject: Performance at Bishop Alderwood's

Dear Robert

You haven't let me know what you think about the proposed programme.

Helen

from: Robert Lyons <rlyons@ArchbishopAlderwood.barnet.sch.uk>
to: Helen Sieger <Helen.Sieger99@gmail.com>
date: 7 May 2014 18:56
subject: Performance at Bishop Alderwood's

Dear Helen

Thank you so much for your helpful email. I'll call you on your mobile but please bear with me as I'm rather snowed under.

Regards

Robert

from: Helen Sieger <Helen.Sieger99@gmail.com>
to: Robert Lyons <rlyons@ArchbishopAlderwood.barnet.sch.uk>
date: 7 May 2014 18:58
subject: Performance at Bishop Alderwood's

Dear Robert

That would be terrific. Do visit Jonty's website in the meantime:

www.jontysieger.com

Helen

from: Helen Sieger <Helen.Sieger99@gmail.com>

to: Fiona Crossley <FRCrossokay@Yahoo.co.uk>

date: 8 May 2014 16:35

subject: FW: The saga comes to an end

Dear Fiona

Am emailing from the wilderness formerly known as our back garden. Had a bit of a contretemps with Boris the gardener and he's refusing to turn up. I can't be bothered pandering to these childish people, so am resigned to doing the weeding myself. (Only one problem - Gerard took all our gardening equipment with him!)

Actually, gardening might help with the stress I've been under. You'll recall my emailing about the problems with Jonty's schools (I didn't hear back btw so am sending again in case you missed it?), well things have taken a definite shift southwards. Mr Lyons has done a complete U-turn vis-à-vis providing opportunities for Jonty. The perfect situation arose with a royal visit to Alderwood's, so I was my usual pro-active self in moving things forward.

It all came to a head today (literally, with the Head phoning me). He said rather tetchily that I might have consulted him on these arrangements. I said this was exactly why I'd called his secretary. He asked why opera arias would be appropriate at the opening of a new sporting facility? I tried to ignore his cheap sarcasm and in my most bright and breezy voice suggested that we might all benefit from taking a day to reflect on the matter. I said I'd stop by after school to discuss things further.

He then dropped a bit of a bombshell. He said he didn't need more time as he'd already discussed the matter at length with his deputy head and two senior teachers. Not sure quite where this leaves the arrangement, so think I'll pop in to clarify very soon.

I would really value a girl's night out – we haven't done that in ages! My mother is quite bonkers as you know (now taping every conversation we have in case I claim to have said anything I didn't.) Oh and Gerard seems to be living in the South of France with a new family. He says it's all "somewhat awkward" and would prefer no contact with Jonty for the time being. Charming!

Bestest

Helen

from: Helen Sieger <Helen.Sieger99@gmail.com>

to: Robert Lyons <rlyons@ArchbishopAlderwood.barnet.sch.uk>

date: 9 May 2014 06:16

subject: Performance at Bishop Alderwood's

Dear Robert

Further to our recent conversation which was most helpful in enabling me to understand your position, I would very much appreciate the opportunity to come in for a meeting. I always feel that a face to face chat is so much more helpful than navigating the perils of email and telephone.

Best regards

Helen

from: Helen Sieger <Helen.Sieger99@gmail.com>

to: Robert Lyons <rlyons@ArchbishopAlderwood.barnet.sch.uk>

date: 9 May 2014 07:02

subject: Performance at Bishop Alderwood's

I should perhaps add that I could rearrange things and attend a meeting at any time today.

Best regards

Helen

from: Helen Sieger <Helen.Sieger99@gmail.com>

to: Robert Lyons <rlyons@ArchbishopAlderwood.barnet.sch.uk>

date: 9 May 2014 17:16

subject: Performance at Bishop Alderwood's

Dear Robert

It has clearly been difficult for you to find time to meet with me today. I was very much hoping to resolve this matter more than a week ahead of the royal visit, but I do have some availability next week. Would it be easier for you to call me on my mobile to arrange?

Helen

Delivery purchases   8 May 2014

Delivery address – confirmed

Helen Sieger

Derry Towers,

Monken Hadley,

Barnet,

Hertfordshire

United Kingdom

Purchase: Transaction ID: 8N6985257X4563828

Seller	Note to seller
Garden Tamers Inc.	You haven't included a note.

Dispatch details

The seller hasn't provided any dispatch details yet

Description	Unit Price	Qty	Amount
EasyLifting truck - 6 Cubic Ft FF	$298.00 USD	1	$298.00 USD
SharpSaw Pruning Saw - 13 in	$64.60 USD	1	$64.60 USD
Rugged-land Rake - 36 in	$75.00 USD	1	$75.00 USD
Garden Power-Mower	$601.80 USD	1	$601.80 USD

Postage and packaging	$0.00 USD
Insurance - not offered	----
Total	$1039.40 USD
Payment	$1039.40 USD

This charge will appear on your credit card statement as "PAYPAL *GARDEN TAMERS"

Payment sent to sales@gardentamers.com

From amount	£636.50 GBP
To amount	$1039.40 USD

Exchange rate: 1 British Pound = 1.63303 US Dollars

1	ROBERT LYONS: Helen, it's Robert from Archbishop
2	Alderwood's. Just clearing my desk on a Saturday so
3	thought I'd give you a ring, err, Helen. Though not sure
4	we have too much to discuss at this point. I believe we've
5	mentioned that the Duchess's visit will be very brief –
6	Kensington Palace is allowing just 15 to 20 minutes. So
7	you'll appreciate there really won't be time for Jonty to
8	provide musical entertainment – though lovely, I'm sure,
9	that would have been from the programme you suggested.
10	What might be useful is for my secretary to contact you
11	to arrange a meeting with Mr Anderson to discuss Jonty's
12	input into the summer concert – this year the 19th June, I
13	think. A lot of the Arias you mentioned would work very
14	well on that occasion, and we could certainly arrange for
15	Jonty to have more time than is usually allotted to soloists.
16	Anyway, Beverly will be in touch. I hope you're having a
17	good weekend and enjoying the sunshine. Many thanks.

CLINICAL NOTES
MR J. BARTHOLOMEW

Mrs Helen Sieger D.O.B. 15.08.74

Address: Derry Towers, Monken Hadley, Barnet, Hertfordshire

Referral date: 10.05.14 Session date: 12.05.14 Session time: 08.40-09.30

Mrs Sieger had telephoned the office to book an appointment at short notice, as "an urgent self referral". Mrs Sieger was offered a recently freed time slot which she gratefully accepted.

Mrs Sieger was an attractive 39 year old Caucasian of medium height, slim build, with wavy brown hair and sallow complexion. She was divorced and had one son, Jonty, aged eleven. She was extremely well dressed, presenting as an articulate and well-educated character of a nervous and volatile disposition. The psychotherapeutic encounter was punctuated with her frequent sighs. Mrs Sieger spoke mostly in a measured manner, but on occasion her voice became constricted by anger.

Mrs Sieger complained that in recent weeks her sleep patterns had been hugely variable: some nights she did not sleep at all. She was preoccupied by two separate strands within her current narrative. The first was the refusal of her son's school to permit him to perform a sequence of arias before the Duchess of Cambridge the following week. This refusal had taken Mrs Sieger by surprise and she spoke about "contacting a barrister" to explore "the human rights angles". Mrs

Sieger seemed incapable of accepting the school's final adjudication on this matter remaining convinced that her reaction was both proportionate and rational. Having said this, Mrs Sieger did venture that following "Mr Lyons' attempts to shovel me across to another teacher", her rage might boil over causing "loss of control". She declined to speculate as to how this might manifest itself.

The other matter troubling Mrs Sieger was the rapid growth of the grass and hedgerows at her home in Monken Hadley. She talked of a "veritable wilderness" since the departure of her most recent gardener. They had had an ill tempered dispute over his use of certain pesticides which Mrs Sieger believed harmful to her son's singing voice. When offered the intervention that the untamed growth of her garden might, for her, be symbolic of a perceived lack of control over her own life, Mrs Sieger smiled broadly and nodded several times.

Mrs Sieger said she found the session helpful and made a further appointment.

Mrs Helen Sieger D.O.B. 15.08.74

Address: Derry Towers, Monken Hadley, Barnet, Hertfordshire

Referral date: 10.05.14 Session date: 19.05.14 Session time: 08.40-09.30

Mrs Sieger did not attend the session, cancel in advance, or explain her absence afterwards. An invoice was duly dispatched to her home address.

from: Beverly Baxter <bbaxter@ArchbishopAlderwood.barnet.sch.uk>

to: Helen Sieger <Helen.Sieger99@gmail.com>

date: 13 May 2014 11.08

subject: Meeting

Dear Ms Sieger,

Mr Lyons has asked me to arrange a meeting with Mr Anderson to discuss Jonty's part in the summer concert. Would you be able to attend at 5 pm this Monday 19th May?

I look forward to hearing from you.

Yours sincerely,

Beverly Baxter

Secretary

1. Whilst on duty with PC Abraham (Mon 19th May) on a 1000-1800 hrs we received a call to attend Bishop Alderwood's school at 1714 in the aftermath of an incident. We understood that one or more persons had been forcibly injured. We were aware of a visit to the school that day of the Duchess of Cambridge. However, this visit had been earlier and was we understood unrelated.

2. PC Abraham and myself were the first officers to arrive at the school, although within a few minutes we had been joined by another ten or twelve officers.

3. We initially attended the school staffroom where a small number of teachers were gathered in a state of some confusion. One teacher took us to a room within the same block where she said a teacher had been meeting a parent. The room was empty but there were distressed shouts from further down the corridor.

4. We arrived at the Head Teacher's office where a MR ANDERSON was attempting to stem the flow of blood from a serious wound in the arm of an injured man in a semi-recumbent position on a soft chair. The injured man appeared to be in danger of passing out. PC Abraham said, "That man needs an ambulance" and we were assured that one had been called and was en-route. We were told that the injured person was the Head Teacher Mr ROBERT LYONS. MR ANDERSON was shouting that HELEN SIEGER had run off. We were informed that HELEN SIEGER, a parent, had come in for a meeting and without provocation had attacked the HEAD TEACHER with a sharp weapon. I requested further background information.

5.   MR ANDERSON strongly suggested that we needed to find MS SIEGER before she attacked somebody else. At this point another individual shouted that MS SIEGER had been seen entering the new gymnasium. I was informed that all children had gone home over half an hour before.

6.   We made our way to the gymnasium on the far side of the site. We were joined by a number of other officers who had just arrived. When we entered the gymnasium 3-4 minutes later, two police officers were restraining a lady who was apparently in a state of some distress. I noticed an implement on the floor of the gymnasium near to the lady. Upon further examination, this was identified as a garden pruning saw.

7.   The lady, MS HELEN SIEGER, was shouting unrelated things, most of which I do not now recall. I believe that she said that she "only picked the stuff up from the post office on my way". She also said that "twenty minutes was plenty of time for a few arrears". By now MS SIEGER was wearing handcuffs and, no longer struggling, was led away to a police van.

8.   Having ascertained that there were no other injured parties and that the situation was now under control and being handled by others, I returned to the station where I recorded this log and completed my shift.

Tonybridge Medical Practice, Tonybridge Way, Barnet EN5 15RD

The Governors
Archbishop Alderwoods School
Eshelby Road
Barnet EN5 14DE

4th October 2014

Dear Sirs,

I write to inform you at the behest of Mr Robert Lyons. As you know, Mr Lyons suffers from Type 2 Diabetes. Following the incident at his school in May, this contributed to the need for an amputation to be performed on the lower part of his left arm. Although Mr Lyons has made an excellent physical recovery from this operation, he continues to suffer from nightmares and is being treated for Post Traumatic Stress Disorder through CBT.

It is my professional opinion that Mr Lyons will not be fit to return to his demanding role as Head Teacher until at least the new year. However, I am continuing to monitor the situation closely.

In my view, a successful prosecution of his attacker may assist his reparative process. I understand that the trial is likely to commence later this year.

Yours sincerely,

Dr R. Hussein

Ms Helen Sieger
Psychiatric Assessment by Dr Dimitrios J Wolfson.
11 October 2014

Summary of conclusions:

1. This report was commissioned to provide an opinion as to whether Ms Sieger has Capacity to plead and take part in her forthcoming criminal trial.

2. It has taken into account Ms Sieger's conduct since she was granted bail on 26.05.14. Ms Sieger has cooperated with medical practitioners and has been taking anti-depressants (Selective serotonin reuptake inhibitors (SSRIs)). She has continued to care for her son Jonty, including overseeing his transfer to a comprehensive school in June.

3. As part of the assessment, Ms Sieger consented to a thorough physical examination being conducted.

4. Ms Sieger is in robust physical health and has no physical disorder which would have any bearing on her ability to plead or understand her trial.

5. Ms Sieger suffers from a Narcissistic Personality Disorder which contributes to her over-developed sense of entitlement and her expectation of receiving special treatment.

6. Ms Sieger was tested under the Beck Depression Inventory and her BDI score indicated a moderate depression.

7. Ms Sieger displayed a full understanding of the charges which she faces. She has taken part in two conferences with her legal team. She understands the adversarial nature of criminal trials.

8. Separately, Mrs Sieger is the subject of a non-molestation order prohibiting further contact with her ex-husband.

9. Ms Sieger has shown interest in the recovery and well being of Mr Robert Lyons and expresses an interest in writing to him. Her legal team is advising on this.

10. Ms Sieger has shown empathy for her son Jonty, who has been deeply affected by the events of this year. She understands his view that music has been the cause of the problems experienced by his family and former school. She regrets his decision to give up singing.

11. In my opinion, Ms Sieger has mental capacity to plead and take part in her criminal trial. The full Psychiatric Report will follow.

Joanna Campbell

Author of Upshots
Winner of the London Short Story Prize 2015

Joanna Campbell's stories are published in The New Writer, Writers' Forum and The Yellow Room and also in collections published by Salt Publishing, Cinnamon Press, Spilling Ink, Earlyworks Press, Unbound Press and Biscuit Publishing. Shortlisted five times for the Bridport Prize and three times for the Fish Prize, she has stories in both the 2010 and 2013 Bristol Short Story Prize Anthologies. In 2011, she came second in the Scottish Writers Association's contest and won the Exeter Writers competition. In 2012 she was shortlisted in Mitchelstown Literary Society's William Trevor/Elizabeth Bowen competition and was the runner-up in 2013. In 2013 she had stories published in both the Salt Anthology of New Writing and also won the local prize in the Bath Short Story Award. Tying Down The Lion, her novel about a 1967 family road-trip to Berlin, was published in June 2015 by Brick Lane. When Planets Slip Their Tracks, her first short story collection, was published in January 2016 in hardback and on Kindle by Ink Tears.

Twitter: @pygmyprose
Website: joanna-campbell.com

Upshots

When the war was on, Da planted a loganberry bush, a scabby cutting from Ma Bandle. She wheels her pram around town, peddling tangled rolls of chicken-wire, encyclopaedias, the odd Indian-head hockey stick—anything she can swap for nosh. There's always a scruffy baby peering out from her mildewed mirrors and smeared candlesticks. Some say a woman-of-the-night once exchanged a child in a fox-fur for a pair of gypsy-hoop earrings, but it's just talk.

Ma Bandle parks the pram under her loganberry bush. Her babies have all stared up at the shovel-shaped leaves and deep-red drooping fruit. The pram hood is stained purple from the bombardment of soft late berries. She says it's the pureness of the bairns that ripens the crop.

In exchange for the cutting, Da handed over Mam's currant loaf. She kicked off when the grape-vine said Ma B had fed it to her hogs. But our bush were worth the sacrifice. It grew to the same height as me—stunted, but still standing. Anyroad, Mam's currant loaf was well-known for bringing on a full day's guts-ache.

"The loganberry were the upshot of a cross-bred raspberry with a blackberry plant," Da said, toeing the soil flat with the tip of his rubber boot. "An accident, like. Two things that weren't meant to cross paths, but turned out all right."

He said any mistake could be put right. It were a matter of sorting out your own mistake, at your own expense and in your own front room.

"Wi' your curtains shut if needs be," he said. "And if owt can't be made tidy, then do away wi' it."

I agreed with owt Da said on account of the way he spoke to me—as slow as cold gravy, knowing me brain-cogs are cock-eyed.

I hear me name spoken like a dog hears a whistle, but the rest of the time, I'm in a world of me own. Da said that were fine, as long as I had a right nice world wi' a roof that didn't leak, a slice of good meat pie, and no women shrieking like banshees in me lughole.

He were a man who righted woodlice when they were spinning on their backs. He sprayed the loganberry leaves with sun-warmed water to soothe their rust blight. He talked to old dogs stretching in pools of sun on the pavement—stray mongrels that is. His face were like a wasp-woozy windfall apple; sun-browned and wind-hardened. He had a gammy leg and other, quiet aches.

I've tried right hard to keep our bush alive. But it caught a rash this summer, a crop of ginger spots, and it's sweating milky stuff. I can't get it well, but I won't do away wi' it neither.

People say I'm slower than a millpond in August, but me big sister Christine's fast. True enough. At the first siren wail, she used to grab her spit-block mascara, a thick heel of bread and the latest Peg's Paper, then shoot down our shelter like a rat up a drainpipe.

When they call her fast though, they mean her legs don't stay crossed as long as they should. Like a pair of drumsticks on a boiling-fowl, the sort that fall apart on Mam's draining-spoon. But when it came to being careful, that's where our Christine lagged behind.

She's just this minute home from the hospital. She and Mam are at the table pretending nowt's happened.

We can't pass the baby off as our Mam's like every other family with a sister fifteen years older than the youngest born, because Mam's insides fell out when she last birthed. I were born like a sunburnt plum, crinkled and navy-blue, our Christine says. More like right browned off, I reckon, but what do I know?

Our Christine's baby's not here. There's a skin-of-milk smell, a worn-out posy of violets I fetched from the florist's floor-sweepings, and black eye-cake smudges on the towel in the scullery. Those things are all here because the baby isn't. There. I worked that out. Took a while. Mam stuffed three ox-hearts for dinner and smoked half a pack of *Park Drive* before I caught on.

When she's back on her feet, our Christine's to have a gold stopper.

"It'll put the smile back on her face," Mam said. "I'm fair itching to see that brass-faced little mare when she sets eyes on it."

The little mare's wed to the stallion—a swarthy streak-of-piddle from MacFisheries, Mam says—who's meant to have Done the Deed. She's also the thrower of the half-pint of stout that chipped our Christine's front tooth. The stout didn't smash it. It were mainly the glass tumbler.

Mam screws her mouth up as tight as a press-stud. "I'd thought you'd learned your lesson, our Christine, but you're still no better than you should be."

It's the kind of wisdom that'd be right dazzling if I could work out what it meant.

Mam's pouring brandy into Christine's tea-dregs, her scowl saying: *Don't-get-used-to-being-spoiled-like-this* and glaring as if it's all our Christine's fault the Bandles are fostering again.

"Ma B will have collected the poor little bugger by now. Wheeling him about, pleased as Punch, she'll be."

Our Christine tries to say, "Shut your gob, Mam," but it sounds like a wedge of seedy cake's clogging her gullet.

"Least said, soonest mended, Mam," I say. It's summat me Da used to come out with, but it never did owt.

"We'll not be wanting your four penn'orth, our Stan," Mam says, trying to belt me ear. She misses, partly on account of being a woman and mostly on account of the Three Barrels bottle being two-thirds empty.

It were a sweltering day like this when me Da dug out the hole for the shelter, his hair stuck to his forehead and his shirt hugging his back. The stuffed hearts wheeze in the oven, steaming up the kitchen while Mam tears newspaper squares for the lavvy. I want to go out to the back yard, but I'm not trusted with me catapult when there's washing on the line, so I stop at the table, lining up me soldiers.

Mam says, "Milk dried up yet, our Christine?"

"Like as not."

"Happen it hasn't, Miss. I can smell it."

"Why d'you blinking well ask me then?"

"I'll get you a lend of a cow-pump."

Our Christine starts sobbing again.

The Bandles live two to a plate, three to a bed, and keep a placid sow in the back room. Our Christine's baby'll lie on a sack in a trough. Nappies sweating in one bin, pig-swill scalding in another. I happen to look up from gluing a boot back on a machine-gunner and see our

Christine's life's worth of tears in her eyes.

Fast she may be, but today our Christine wants to stop the clock and be back in the hospital. Or die.

Doodlebugs upset her. Not the racket, but the sudden silence of the engine cutting out, its trek through the sky over.

While it plummeted, she'd clutch me jummy sleeve like she was wringing out the woollens on wash-day. Her red-painted talons hurt enough to take me mind off the V-1.

"Oh, Stan, it's our turn, isn't it? This one's for us," she'd say.

"I'd look and see if it's got our name on," I'd say, cocky-like. "Only it's dark as pitch out there, our Christine, and they don't call me Speccy Four-Eyes on account of me night-vision."

That were me being right quick.

"I'm going to wet meself, Stan."

You'd never think she were sixteen years older than me.

"Just knot your legs together."

If only she'd heeded that advice when the war was over.

Mam calls the baby a little duck, a hip-splitting ten-pounder and a poor little bleeder, but whatever his name is, I feel right sad for him wi'out his Mam. Ours might be as much use as a jelly pencil, but at least we've got one.

It's not only our Christine's hips that are torn asunder—not that I can tell what with her still wearing a frock made from two bed-sheets. Her soul's in pieces too. Not just from blasting out the ten-pounder, but from rattling home round the bomb-craters on the thirty-seven bus—still on half-fare—wi' nowt.

Stop the clock a minute. I'm thinking.

Well, cover me in batter and fry me in dripping, I've been slower than slurry. It's obvious what happens next.

I'm thinking loganberries. A cross-bred plant. An accident. But summat good came of it in the end. It nearly turns me brain inside-out, but I make me mind up. This time I bleedin' well *will* go out and find what's got our name on it.

It won't actually have 'Grimshaw-originally-from-Yorkshire' printed on a label, but nor did any Doodlebugs. The world and his wife already know what our Christine's been up to, so why bother if he comes to live at ours? The little blighter deserves his rightful name. Any mistake can be put right.

I gather up the machine-gunner and some kneeling soldiers with rifles. When our Christine sees me next, I'll be holding the best present she's ever had. Worth a whole cakehole full of gold teeth.

The Bandles live round the block, past the bombed-out shops and tumbledown church, messy and in danger of collapse. I pass a closing-down sale and think of shop-soiled goods and fallen women.

I still can't make the connection between having a baby and being a dirty little scrubber. If you scrub, you're a sight cleaner than our Christine. She's always last in the line when the tub comes out, then squawks about not setting a toe in our grime. On her birthday she gets sixpence for the public washrooms and has her own slipper-bath. Mam says the water must fetch up blacker than the ace-of-spades. And I say wouldn't it be better to take the slippers off first.

Along the riverbank, past the wasteland and over the bridge to the playing-field, round the back lanes and past the school that isn't there anymore, and I'm fair out of breath. Me feet are soaked through on account of slipping into the river twice. One of the privates in me pocket jabs me leg with his rifle, but I'm too busy thinking to be bothered.

Clammy and shaky, I drop onto the half-bench, the only thing left here apart from a poorly horse-chestnut that used to rain down conkers and the brass school-bell minus its clapper. A blackbird tugs a worm out of the ground, stretching it tight until it snaps and, like the worm, makes do with the half he's got.

I see Ma Bandle with her pram.

One wheel squawks like a toad is trapped in the tyre. The coachwork, once cream and red, is shabby and peeling. It's housed ten Bandle babies and an assortment of others she takes on, like the caterpillars I used to collect in a jam-jar. But today, bumping over the cobblestones, is Our Baby. And if I know me arse from me elbow, I know where Ma Bandle is heading—Pig Club.

A group of people set it up in the war, all chipping in to keep the animals in the school field and fatten them up with scrapings. It's well known the Bandles don't stump up many scraps, but they scramble to the front of the queue when it's time to dish out the bacon. The war might be over, but Pig Club's not been given the chop and Mrs Bandle still expects her rashers.

She parks the pram, hikes up her skirts and clambers over the barbed wire to the hanging-room. Beneath the branches buckling under brown-tinged blossom, I'm not even a shadow.

I start to run, but she bustles back with her basket and leans over the pram, murmuring away as always. Leastways I can give her one less gob to feed. She takes out a pile of stuff for barter and sets out for the hanging-room again.

For a four-eyed lad, I move as quick as hell can grill an ounce of cheese. Flying to the pram, I rummage through the bric-a-brac, snatch the baby in its blanket and scram. Our Christine fast? She's got nothing on me today.

But running home under a thickening sky with an almighty stitch in me side and a bongo-drum in me head, I stop.

Mam'll take one look and kick off.

But I think of our Christine's eyes, the same as me Da's the last time I saw him. And I'm buggered if I'm taking it back.

In me head, I hear a hammer-clanging, drum-banging, bucket-clanking din. Me skin's blistering like a flame-split tomato. I don't know how one foot finds itself in front of the other, but somehow I'm in our back yard. The blanket's the weight of a boulder. Me arms become two ribbons.

Hail thrashes the dustbin like a downpour of hob-nails. Me head knows I must keep the baby safe and dry, but me body's just standing here beside the bin, the empty rabbit-hutch, the broken mangle, the rusting bed-head.

"Make it tidy," Da said. "Or do away wi' it."

Stumbling along, me specs rain-fogged, I reach the end of the yard, the pink of the child's cheek glistening between the folds of the blanket. I stagger down the sandbag slope and tug at the ragged tin door of the shelter. It scrapes on the ground before it gives in.

Deep inside the cool earth, I place the bundle on the bench where our Christine used to sit bolt upright. "Lean on me," I'd say.

I stand me best rifleman next to the babe. And I want to lay meself down too.

Bleedin' hell, I need me mam right bad.

I reel into the kitchen.

A duet of screams. A scattering of tea-cups.

Me arms are smothered in rust-red blight. A canopy of swivelling black spots, sick-skinny creepers, tattered leaves bleed over me, their tarnished colours too early for autumn.

The kitchen spins.

German measles is a three-week canker.

The air is blotched with calico-mosaic disease. I need well-irrigated soil. I'm parched, weakening, disappearing through the loam-mattress, curling round the tendril-springs, slipping through the root-tangled, fluff-packed floorboard gaps, coiling into the earth.

When me bed is drenched with sweat and me thrashing legs wear snags in the sheet, I'm transferred to our Christine's. She watches me through her cigarette smog.

"He's smiling in his sleep. Look Mam," she says. "Turning the corner now."

I keep turning corners. Expectant, sweating, sandy-tongued, I run on, searching. I hear creaking, squeaking wheels in me head. I wake up to Christine spooning medicine into me or reading aloud from a story paper, one of the tuppenny-bloods.

I strengthen. The soil loosens. I feel it shift. I stretch into the cool, lengthening space.

At the end of the third week, a navel orange perched on the sill glows like a small, zesty sun. The white sails of the windblown curtains surge, billowing the air clean, and the door opens wide, unfolding the cramped floor-shadows into long, straight bars.

Braced by a pile of winter coats for extra pillows and our Christine's shawl round me shoulders, I sit up to skin the orange, shedding peel into

33

the candlewick channels, the juice scoring through the stench of sickness.

"Happen God knew we'd lost enough already, Mam," I hear our Christine say down in the kitchen.

She means our Da. He went tending the dead after the V-1 blast. He saw Ma Bandle's own child. It was blown from her arms into the fireplace. A bomb and a baby—two things that weren't never meant to cross paths, but didn't turn out all right. It couldn't be made tidy. It had no face after.

Da came home, but he weren't here. He sat by the range, listening to the coals changing places, one cheek well basted because he didn't move for hours.

"Some days, Mam, me arms hurt that bad for want of holding 'im," Christine says.

One night after that last explosion, our Da went out. He kept on walking in the pitch dark until his shoes wore through. I know that because a man with a fox-terrier found them side by side on the river bank.

"Leastways your milk's gone now," Mam says, her thumb pressing a foil bottle-top that hisses as it caves in.

"Thank God. It weighed a whole stone on its own. But I miss him, Mam."

"What's done is done, our Christine. No point crying over spilt… you know."

"Will it always hurt like this, Mam?"

"Aye. Like hell, love. But you've to get on with it."

"Can't I have him back?"

"You know fine well the shame would kill me this time. And at least you've still got the lad. Pulled through his measles, didn't he? Isn't that enough?"

I hear this, but I don't listen to the words. Me heart's an express train pumping through an empty station. I hear the kettle and the teaspoons, the moist thud of a knife through fruit cake, and I know something.

Our Christine's not talking about me Da.

Someone else has gone.

Someone else is missing.

Hidden in a blanket.

I throw back the sheet. Orange peel scraps and half me tin militia fly across the room. The tuppenny-bloods cascade to the floor. I stand up and fall over, not used to being upright. I cram two legs in one trouser hole. Can't find me shoes. Me specs are still spotted with powdery-white rain.

"What's going on up there?" Mam shouts.

"Need a wee!"

I fall over again, in shock at me quick thinking.

"Use the gazunder."

"No, I'm better!"

"You're weak as a kitten, lad."

"Honest, Mam. I'll go in the privy and straight back."

"Quick as ninepence then."

Outside the laundry hangs heavy. Mam yells, "And watch that clean linen, lad," while I tussle with the wall of wet flannelette.

I look back at them peering at me and see the golden flash of our Christine's new smile.

I stumble down the yard, listening. Shouldn't there be wailing? A bit of a grizzle?

Nothing.

It'll be right fine though. Babies are tough as old boots.

Mam opens the window.

"Think on, lad. You've grown that skinny you'll fall down the hole."

I haven't felt like eating. Just sleeping, dreaming, scratching, sweating. Maybe the baby's had German measles as well. I'll dose it with what's left of me medicine later.

Mam and our Christine's voices float out with their cigarette smoke.

"I saw Ma Bandle when I went for our Stan's orange, Mam. The pram was loaded up. An old clock, a pair of boots with no laces. I didn't look in though, Mam."

A bird pecks at something in the hot dirt near me bare feet.

Fallen fruit.

The bush has lost its carroty spots. The leaves aren't curling over in prayer. The berries are dusky-red, bloated with juice. I pick one. It stains the palm of me hand a beautiful purple-black. It bleeds over me tongue.

"Not far from bush to dish now," Da used to say.

I think of hot loganberry-pie wi' a splash of top-o'-the-milk.

"There, there, love," Mam says to Christine.

I walk on, me soles rasping on the concrete. Everything looks foreign through the greasy haze of me glasses. It were this bright the day they found Da. I wondered how the sun could still be there.

I look up in case Da might be showing hisself in the moon; I always watch the full moon, the half-moon, the moon with bits nibbled off to see if he's there. But he never is.

I stop at the shelter. I can't hear them talking anymore, not properly. The odd word drifts down when Mam goes back and forth to the windy-sill where she keeps the matches and the pot of used tea-leaves, and the blurry little snap she took of our Christine's baby.

The tin door is too stiff to open. I put me ear against it.

Nothing.

I hear me name, and its echo.

A rag-and-bone man shouts from the main road.

Hoofs clatter by.

A cup chinks on a saucer in next-door's garden.

A bird flaps in the long grass around the shelter, its dark wings draping over the clover. After fussing for a while, it folds them back in.

Me fingers quiver when I try to push the door.

Four tries before it gives.

Inside, the sun has turned the bone-cool, fresh root smell into the reek of a roasting oven with summat forgotten inside. The stench stops me breathing. I leave the door open, one hand over me mouth. Even me rifleman's fainted.

I step towards the small bundle on the bench where I left it. Of course! The nappy will be full o' shite by now. That'll be what's kicking up the stink.

Except this is not that kind of pong.

It's like right rancid, half-baked meat; the rotting, crawling kind.

Maggoty-bad.

I peel back the blanket, just a little.

Close up, the reek is ten times worse.

This babe doesn't look pure enough to bring on a crop of ripe berries.

I hear me name.

Can't see much in here. I can make out a lumpy mottled pattern speckled over flesh that's not as pink as it should be. More silvery-green.

The bundle is heavy, but quite, quite still. Sod it, the poor bleeder's gone and taken ill with loganberry-canker in exchange for ripening me bush.

I hear me name.

I wish I could run to the river, slice through its calm skin and puncture the never-ending dark. Leave me shoes on the bank. Neat like.

But I have to go inside.

Dragging me black-soled feet, I pass our bush, looking tired now with its burden of hot fruit. Happen I cared for it too well.

Drifts of conversation puff through the air.

"She got kicked out of Pig Club the other week, did you hear, Mam?"

"Why's that, love?"

"The foreman reckoned she swiped a ham hock."

I stand on the door mat, eyes streaming. Tears won't get me any gold teeth. Happen a gobful of broken ones instead.

"Oh, go on. Did she really, our Christine?"

"Aye, she really did. Swore blind she were overcome with shame and about to hand over half her worldly goods in fair exchange. Said some bugger must have sneaked up and nicked it out the pram."

I step inside.

"A whole bloody ham hock? Well I never, our Chrissy. Well, I never."

They turn to me.

"In God's name, what have you got there, lad?"

"Oh, our Stan," Christine shrieks. "It stinks to high bleedin' heaven. What the hell…?"

Happen me and this bundle weren't meant to cross paths.

I get two clips round the ear, one from each of 'em.

I want to say I'd like our small lad back. He'll be staring up at Ma Bandle's shovel-shaped leaves now, watching the sky, waiting for her to lift him up and take him inside. But I keep that thought to meself, take the trug and go back with Mam and our Christine to gather fruit.

Gary Budden

Author of Saltmarsh

Gary Budden is the co-founder of independent publisher Influx Press and an editorial assistant at Unsung Stories.

His work has appeared in Structo, Elsewhere, Unthology, Gorse, The Lonely Crowd, Galley Beggar Press, Brittle Star and many more. His pamphlet Tonttukirkko was published by Annexe in 2014.

He writes regularly for Unofficial Britain and blogs about landscape punk, weird fiction and more at newlexicons. blogspot.co.uk He lives in London.

Twitter: @gary_budden

Saltmarsh

In the city he sees mainly i) green parakeets swarming in the trees of Gladstone Park ii) rot-legged pigeons the colour of exhaust fumes peppering the sky above Staples Corner and iii) jays that flit colourfully among the trees near the Jewish cemetery. The first two he hates, and the third he has a real fondness for.

It's holiday season and the marsh grass is jaundiced and sullen. Simon has left the boatyard behind, with its creaking rusted winches, fleece-wearing woodcutters and carved folk art, where boats bob on the creek with names like *Jack Orion, Georgie* and *Reynard*. Now he is thankfully alone, the town that fades out by the creek falling away behind him. The cold needles his skin and the sky is the blue of a blackbird's egg. The wind is sharp like flint. Electricity pylons march towards the murky waters of the Swale. The sunlight exposes all.

Yesterday, over a bad Skype connection, Simon's sister relayed breathy accounts of seeing not one, but two sea eagles in as many weeks on the broads between Norfolk and Lowestoft. A train rumbling through morning mist, sharp talons and a yellow beak. (She meant the white-tailed eagle). He has never seen a sea-eagle (white-tailed eagle) bar on his HD screen with a BBC presenter relaying the facts, figures and opinions. He is jealous of his sister for this, feels it's a sight that should be earned. It's not a bird for amateurs. He knows that to give himself the chance of even seeing such a bird he needs to be elsewhere; not in the city, not in the south-east trudging through this saltmarsh. Though in this county, at the right time of year, he knows he can see the harriers with talons locked tight together spiralling down into the reeds at Stodmarsh. It's a sight that opens up parts of him not normally accessible. This year, he promises himself, he will take Adrianna to see them. They are rare and it hurts him to watch them.

Once he and Adrianna saw, through a smeared bus window, a white peacock treading the tarmac somewhere near Regents Park, disrupting the traffic. He wonders briefly what happened to it and remembers the confused honking of the taxi drivers. Whether they were heading towards, or coming back from Victoria he can't remember.

He is not in East Anglia yet the landscape here is similar. Intimidating flatness with too much space for the mind to wander. The haunting burble of curlews out on the mudflats, affecting still despite the amount written about them. A boat of some sort (he's not a sailor) nose-down in the creamy mud as if burrowing for lugworms. These are not broads though, this patch between Faversham (his point of departure) and Whitstable (destination). What constitutes a 'broad', Simon wonders? Something to look up.

Seven miles ahead lies the fishing-cum-tourist town where, he knows, the cafes are already full (they have names like *Samphire*) and the pubs (*Neptune*, *The Ship Centurion*) are filling up, glasses stamped with the Shepherd Neame logo sloshing with amber liquid. He can already taste that pint, the pleasing decision between Spitfire, Whitstable Bay or Bishop's Finger. A bag of scampi fries too. It will be well-earned, the fractal patterns of mud that flow up his trousers the mark of honour to say, 'I have earned this drink'. It's a personal thing. Goals are important, no matter how arbitrary.

If you asked why he is out here on this saltmarsh, he would be hard pressed to come up with an answer. He just feels the compulsion these days to connect town to town by foot, no car, bike or train providing enough significance. Slowing. Progressing.

To come into a new town on foot, the buildings slowly coalescing and condensing into a form that can be slapped with a useful postcode, is one of life's rarest pleasures. Sometimes an explanation is not needed when the truth is self-evident. He feels it, and therefore (for him at least) it is true. He'd like to think he's part of some form of mild rebellion. He's been trying to persuade John to come with him on one of these trips.

It does sound good when announced in pubs back in the city, where the perceptions of rural, provincial, anything other than exhaust fume and clogged carriage, is deemed luxurious and exotic. Simon once announced, half-cut on a Kentish ale now sold in London arts venues, 'I am being throttled by the M25'.

Adrianna hates his grandiose statements, but she dreams idly of leaving too. She thinks maybe the West Country, trips to the Mendips and Deer Leap, supping cider in Bath or Bristol. They've considered coming back to the somehow overcrowded rural parts of Kent; they both have family here. Simon feels the appeal, yet doesn't believe he can be one of *those people*. Maybe somewhere on the Sussex coast with the blue waters of the channel and local mackerel in a bun? Right now anywhere else would do. Home is no longer no home.

Home is a place where the skyline is stabbed by cranes, bent as if in prayer, diggers like mastodons whose wheels are slathered in London clay, half-built or half-demolished buildings (he finds it hard to tell these days) that he'd describe as skeletons or shells if he could consider anything living ever using them.

He and his friends, Adrianna who he thinks of as his wife but not his wife, are now cash and time poor. He resents that a few drinks with John on a Wednesday night can set him back as much as thirty quid. Resenting the cost of your spare time, a terrible thing.

He says he's forgotten how to live in anywhere other than the cramped metropolis, and that, perhaps, is why he is here on these cold salt-marshes when he could instead be at home with Adrianna, in bed sipping coffee and reading the arts section of the *Guardian*.

The wind stings his eyes. Two polite cyclists, mud spinning off their wheels like a Catherine wheel, say 'hello' and 'good morning' politely as they pass Simon on their way (he assumes) for a brunch and coffee in one of the new boutique cafes of Faversham creek. They recede into the distance and Simon stops to look at, and photograph, a green, white and wasp coloured Environment Agency sign attached to metal fencing warning of the numerous ways to die out here: unguarded culverts, deep water, slippery surfaces, deep mud, underwater obstructions, etc.

Simon wonders, briefly, where and when samphire grows (and how to cook it) and wishes he could identify the sullen plant life he's stamping on. If only I had a garden, he thinks, then I could begin to get to grips with all this. He wants the feel of seed in his hand before he lets it fall on fertile earth. Would the parakeets back home eat that scattered seed? Hopefully not. He has a book on organic gardening, in a bag underneath the spare bed, along with his old copies of *Magnesium Burns* and *Punk Positive* that he never reads but cannot let go of.

This garden in his mind has a simple birdbath, discreet nesting boxes nailed to the tree (his garden needs at least one tree, preferably fruiting, preferably apple) and a squirrel proof feeder to attract dunnocks and goldfinches. He plans on a ceramic recreation of the face of the green man, placed somewhere to surprise the visitor when their eyes finally alight on it. He would also like a Sheela-na-gig (though visitors may find the exaggerated vulva off-putting).

His garden would also contain one of those tinkly metal things that chime in the breeze. That could be good. Simon thinks of his favourite animals i) narwhal/sea-unicorn ii) chocolate and butterscotch pine marten and iii) simple umber fox/Reynardine. If motifs of these animals could be woven into the design of his garden, all the better. Adrianna mocks what she calls his 'hippy shit', and he can see her point.

Once, at a festival somewhere in a field outside of Winchester (where he and Ade met Jess) he saw a gypsy/traveller type selling wicker women in figures of restful repose, a gaia-type addition to any flower bed. He found them rather striking, but thought it best to keep his thoughts to himself. Could see Adrianna's piss-take face and could hear John's condemnation. Simon is getting older and listens to more and more music featuring acoustic guitars and fiddles. He watches *Springwatch* with a passion, and the number of jumpers he owns is increasing. He never thought he'd go this way, but finds it all strangely pleasing.

At present, he knows little about soil rotation, whether his loam and humus would be alkali or acid, and wonders if eggshell really is a good addition to a compost mulch. What is the best brand of shovel, trowel, fork? He feels a kind of hatred towards the mild mannered TV presenters of the BBC (one of whom, he discovered, moonlights as a successful romance novelist). Simon doesn't want to be one of those English people, discussing the merits of different brands of bonemeal in provincial garden centres, in a county where the St George's cross flaps constantly in the wind. But he does want a garden.

He can see a number of false starts, but the journey, not the destination, is the point, right?

So much to learn.

He likes to find areas of mild interest but nothing to shout about, then connect the two by footpaths seldom trod. Photograph the burrowing boats and rusting detritus obscured by reeds. Upload the pictures to a Wordpress-hosted blog, along with a modest amount of text. Share amongst other landscape enthusiasts (there are many online behind their computers in cramped flats). He is part of, he supposes, a kind of community.

The curlew calls again. He pauses, checks his phone. Buzzings and exclamation marks concerning some breaking outrage. A message from Adrianna wishing he has a good day and asking what time he thinks he may be home. She's only back in Faversham; they are staying with her parents for the holiday period. He'll hop on the train back (about a five-minute trip) later on. There are a few favourites and one retweet for the picture of the Environment Agency sign he's uploaded to Twitter. He theorises his use of the word 'culvert' helped in this.

He is walking now at a steady pace, his face bitten by the wind but sweating slightly inside his thick green coat. Simon walks parallel to a narrow strip of water, the Swale, separating here (mainland) from there (Isle of Sheppey). Over there are prisons, boxing hares, economic hardships and stories of monsters in the reeds. Somewhere on the island is the skull of Grey Dolphin (a horse).

There are approximately 5,000 islands dotted around the coast of the UK. As he walks along the Swale, Simon counts all the islands he has visited:

i) Scilly Isles with dad, aged 9/10, approx. 1989; St Mary's, Tresco, Samson. Helicopter journey from Penzance.

ii) Isle of Wight, rained-out camping trip with Adrianna, 2011.

iii) Farne Islands, aged 11/12, dad again, approx. 1991, memorable for being dive-bombed by nesting terns and watching bridled guillemots.

iv) Lindisfarne? Will check with dad. He remembers an abbey, somewhere.

v) Isle of Sheppey, tracking Grendel and Grey Dolphin. Boxing hares on the fields.

vi) Vartiosaaari, off the coast of Helsinki. Adrianna found very affecting, 2012. Picked wild blueberries, watched mating great crested grebes and found a troll church.

vii) Suomenlinna (originally Sveaborg/Viapori); inhabited ex-seafort off Helsinki. Chain of six islands in total, formally Swedish defence against the Russians. A restaurant where Adrianna gingerly ate reindeer.

viii) Isle of Dogs (of course).

ix) Fish Island, East London (named after surrounding streets Bream, Roach, Dace etc). They used to like to drink down that way, before things changed.

x) Isle of Man, sometime during early teens. Indistinct memory of a cat with no tail and watching black guillemots through a new pair of binoculars that dad had bought him for Christmas.

Not a stunning list, but it could be worse.

He and John have a plan, of sorts, to find passage to Dead Man's Island in the estuary, lying just off Sheppey. The difficulty in getting there is becoming part of the point – the pointless pilgrimage – almost every aspect of it becoming the cliché of some hoary old ghost story. They have to arrange private passage with a local fisherman, who will take them to the island, as well as securing permission from Natural England. It's a bird sanctuary built on disease and suffering. The place appeals to his curiosity and John's morbidity. They want to find the diseased bones of the dead Frenchmen rising from the mud. Remnants of the prison hulks (whose inmates he can only ever picture as Ray Winstone in a BBC Dickens adaptation). And so on. He knows his Twitter followers would go nuts for it. Adrianna finds it macabre and is not interested.

Simon passes on the path a group of men and women, six in total, swilling strong lager from cans that bear the image of a European bison (wisent).

They speak a language that may indeed be Polish but he is hopelessly unsure. He wants to ask them what they're up to (in a friendly way) but decides against it. Attempts a 'good morning' like with the cyclists back near Faversham, but is met with silence. They continue until the saltmarsh swallows them and they disappear from view. A herring gull shrieks.

Simon pauses to lean against the concrete flood defence that borders this part of the path, rolls and lights a cigarette. He looks over the waters of the Swale to Sheppey. The water is choppy, the colour of silt and slate, freezing. He feels the desire to push on, to be back among eating drinking people and out of the stinging wind. The sun is blinding him and he wishes he'd brought sunglasses like Adrianna suggested.

By his feet he notices a few orange-brown mushrooms pushing up through the grass. Another thing to add to his list: mycology. Wouldn't it be nice to forage the occasional meal, with the added danger of vomiting and stomach cramps.

The curlew cries, like bubbles escaping from a mouth submerged.

He is meeting John in the pub. His oldest friend is also down in Kent visiting family. It's that time of year.

Though they often see each other in London, this is a good excuse for Simon to do this walk, stretch the legs and mind, and to sit in the warmth of his favourite pub, The Old Neptune, sipping Shepherd Neame ale by a crackling fire, listening to the Irish landlord and looking at the glass containers of pickled whelks sitting behind the bar. No one ever seems to buy them. Often, the hippy ex-road-protester guy, Fen, can be found propping up the bar. Fen lived in a friend's shed for a decade and wrote a book (self-published) suggesting the UK is, in fact, a buried giant. Or a cherubic being in flight (if you look hard). Whitstable is the centre of the Gog-Magog axis, Fen says on the videos on his YouTube channel. It sounded good but sadly, Simon realised, probably didn't mean much.

Sun reflects like quicksilver off of the mudflats that look carved from stone. Simon pauses to examine a sign. The bird and plant life to be found here on South Swale nature reserve. Brent geese, buntings, red breasted mergansers.

Above him tower the pylon's domineering sexual pose. He thinks he hears a crackling sound.

He walks with no other humans in sight. A luxury to be alone on this packed island.

A pub, lonely out here on the marshes, takes form. The Shipwrights Arms, famous in local lore for its spectral-star, the ship spectre. The ghosts here crowd and whisper like the reeds.

It's a pub he has never, in fact, visited. Too local, he used to assume, but perhaps this trip will be the time that he ventures in there. With mud spattered trousers, binoculars and thick green coat it seems more acceptable somehow, rather than settling down with a pint and crisps as an obvious Londoner. Or DFL (Down From London) as they are known.

Even though Simon grew up around here, technically no DFL, he feels disconnected from the place. So, perhaps, this walk is an act of penance, a pilgrimage in a secular age. He could have driven, after all (about fifteen minutes) or gotten the train (service every half hour, five-minute journey time), whereas this walk will take, roughly, four hours.

On foot, the world becomes a bigger place. To be in the places you only normally stare at through the train window feels revelatory. Like stepping into the background somehow, text tumbling over the margin and off the page, wading into the painting, whatever; it's that feeling of being *elsewhere* that is so compelling. And finding *elsewhere* at home? He never thought it possible.

He trudges on. Out on the water bobs a boat so rusted it cannot possibly be in use. Back at the creek he'd looked at the boats clearly inhabited, rainbow-coloured, evoking the lyrics of folk songs. Who were these people?

He's heard the stories about the raves on the marshes. His younger cousin Teddy has done it. An eight-mile schlep back home through mud and mire, still pilled up and happy as the summer sun came up over Sheppey. Simon envies him.

Though didn't he do just the same? Just in different places. He thinks of home that is becoming not home, and a real pang grips his insides. Bits of that life that he does not regret, but that he cannot return to, come in a tidal flood:

i)   London Bridge, summertime, dawn. The sight of the sun appearing to light the Thames. The breath-taking moment when he truly knew where he was, and he was in London.

ii)   Visiting the Cable Street mural with Adrianna for the very first time; drizzle in the air and grey skies and a bit of tiny pride in this city that was home.

iii) Him and his old friend Sally, in the wooded outskirts of a festival near Northampton, high as kites and swearing in the trees they could discern anthropoid figures; wodewose, spriggan, green man, etc.

iv) An impromptu picnic with Adrianna in Springfield Park. Summer drizzle forcing them to take shelter under foliage. Orthodox Jewish wedding at one end of the park, lads dealing weed at the other.

They sipped cava from plastic flutes and ate humus with Turkish bread.

v)   The Balustrade, NYE 2003.

Simon, Adrianna, John – though they've knocked it on the head now, they're all au fait with what goes in these marginal spaces. Psy-trance and drum n bass in the woods in Wiltshire. Heavy bass and bowel-churning dub up in the Brecon Beacons. Countless nights of piercings, dreadlocks and heavy, heavy hardcore in The Balustrade.

The path begins slowly to become more and more regulated, the buildings of the small hamlet of Seasalter appearing. He walks for a good two miles along the bleak shoreline thinking not of the place where he is now, in winter in biting wind, but of a place that no longer exists, in a past that he misses.

The Balustrade up in east London is long gone, bulldozed and converted into i) luxury flats ii) a franchise coffee shop and iii) an 'arts' space. Its destruction was one of those nails in the coffin that has made him and Adrianna consider jumping ship.

The place where he and John spent many, many nights, where Simon met Adrianna, a place that he wishes still exists. It *was* an arts space, a creative space, a space for people. But not the right kind of people. Untaxable and in the way of progress.

Which means he and the woman he loves were not, and possibly are not, the right kind of people. Simon always felt all those commonplace emotions as a young man; I don't fit in, the world is not for me, I feel an outcast, etc. It always seemed too obvious a point to give any serious contemplation. Out here, on the edges of this saltmarsh, covered in mud and listening to the burbling of the curlew, it feels correct. If he is being strangled by the M25, then his memories of the city are now being bulldozed and redeveloped.

His phone buzzes in his pocket and snaps him back into the moment. Sometimes his leg spasms even when there is no phone there, when no one is trying to contact or communicate with him. It's one of those modern things, John assures him. This one is real though.

"Here Now," from John.

"Twenty minutes," Simon replies.

Simon picks up the pace, a slight dampness now under the armpits that he enjoys and considers honest. He passes what look like the tyre treads for a tank rusting next to silent beach huts with names like Oystercatcher and Curlew Cottage. A few houses jut up onto the beach itself and he crunches across the pebble and shingle to pass them. A Union Jack flutters high up a white pole. Simon shakes his head.

He can feel a new town beginning to take shape. Dog walkers begin to appear, a pair of young and eager joggers jog past, older couples arm in arm brace against the wind as they take a walk. Back to reality.

He passes the golf course and thinks, as always, how the land should be taken and rewilded. Give it back to the curlews and turnstones, take it from the men with silly trousers.

Finally, the pub comes into view. Isolated outpost against the sea. The Old Neptune. Simon has been drinking here on and off for twenty years now and it still is his favourite.

He pushes the door, steps inside. Warmth and that wonderful smell of lager and human beings hits him. The fire is going and John has commandeered a table to make full use of the warmth. Above the fire is a stylised portrait of Ian Dury.

"Took your time," says John with a grin. He's been ripping beermats.

"What are you having?" Simon asks.

*

Old Fen sits at the bar dreaming of the fallen giant that lies beneath Kent. The Irish barmaid polishes glasses, pickled shellfish preserved behind her in glass containers.

Simon and John clink their pint glasses in greeting. Outside the sky is still sharp and clear. Simon can see a few gulls pecking at a discarded and congealing bag of chips out on the stones. The tide is out, flat mud stretching towards Sheppey. Beyond that, over the estuary, Southend, Essex, the rest of England.

"Good walk?" asks John. He wears a new Fred Perry Harrington, gleaming boots, dark blue jeans.

"Yeah, it was good, gets the blood pumping and all that."

"It's nice being down here, even at this time of year. I do miss it at times."

"Me too. But I think we forget all the reasons why we left."

"The Union Jacks and the boredom."

"We couldn't wait to get away, remember? The fucking small town bullshit. All we did was burn wood on the beach and smoke ourselves stupid and plan trips up to London."

"At least we had the beach."

"We did."

They sit and talk for a few hours, cocooned in the warmth of the pub, of how each other's families are doing, of how Adrianna is, how John is doing since his breakup. How Old Fen has propped up the bar since as long as they can remember. There's a gig coming up in London that they plan to be at, the last night at The Stockwell Arms before the developers are let loose. They laugh and make light of it. Neither admits the discomfort they feel. These places, these are their shared stories.

"Remember The Balustrade?" says John, booze fuelling nostalgia.

"Fucking hell what a place," says Simon.

"Where you met Ade wasn't it?"

"Yeah."

And Simon thinks how twelve years have passed and how the present became the past. He wants to tell his friend about his ideas for gardens, about the trips to the Mendips he has yet to take yet that are so vivid in his mind they feel like cherished memories, how he needs to get out of the city, change, move on, before the whole world he knew gets knocked down. It all sounds like so much bitter moaning when aired; and as such, often, the conversation remains perfunctory. They retell stories of the things they did and struggle to imagine what they now will do.

John gets up, stretches his arms and rubs a hand over his cropped hair, and heads to the bar for another pint. He flirts with the Irish barmaid. He has a charisma that Simon has always envied. The pub is filling up with Kentish locals, an old man with an old dog, gleaming middle-class couples who must be down, like them, from the city. The fire crackles.

Old Fen smiles to himself and sips his pint.

Author of Partitions

Stephanie Scott was born in Singapore. She read English Literature at York and Cambridge and worked in Investment Banking in New York, London and Rome, before leaving finance to write full-time. Her debut novel, The Sentence, is set in modern Japan and she won the A.M. Heath Prize for her novel in manuscript form, a Distinction for her MSt in Creative Writing at Oxford, The Toshiba Studentship in 2012, the Arvon Jerwood National Fiction Award in 2013 and the Writers Centre Norwich Inspires Award in 2014 also for her novel.

Thus far, Stephanie's short fiction has focused on South East Asia where she grew up: a poem on the Death Railway in Thailand was a winner of the Fish International Poetry Prize 2011, her prose on the bombing of Hiroshima was shortlisted for the Bridport Prize 2012, 2013 and 2014, and her fiction on the partition of India has been shortlisted for the Glimmer Train International Short Fiction Award and the Mslexia Short Story Award 2014. Stephanie was most recently published in the February 2015 issue of Mslexia.

Twitter: @stephaniewscott

Stephanie Scott

Partitions

When I think of 1947, I remember the rain. In Lahore, when the clouds gather and darken, the rain falls in dense drops to the ground sending up puffs of red dust. The earth turns into streams, then rivers of clay that course through the storm drains of the city. It was during rainfall such as this that Haamid returned to the house on Mehmood Street. Water droplets were scattered in his hair and his leather sandals were caked in mud. There is no way of escaping our country; it will hold you, imprint itself on your skin.

My family are Hindus from Bahawalpur, where the plains of Cholistan meet the undulating walls of the Derawar Fort. I had been coming to the house on Mehmood Street ever since I was a little girl, ever since Joshna and I started boarding school together. My mother was educated at Armitage College under the Raj and she had met my Auntie Aisha there in a mixed dorm. Today, I can still see them: two girls, one Hindu, one Muslim, their clothes piled onto the same chair - a Punjabi dupatta, a hijab, two pleated plaid skirts - about to embark upon a friendship that would extend to their daughters. For every year, between the summer and autumn terms, instead of travelling the many days home to the desert, I lived with Joshna and her family in Lahore.

We were sewing when Haamid returned that day; I had been listening for his footsteps on the marble. The rain pattered softly on the tiles as the front door opened and closed. All through the summer, I had found no notes from him in the women's quarters; he no longer waited for me on the roof at dusk. That afternoon, Joshna watched me as I listened to Haamid remove his sandals and walk up the stairs. He did not join us as he would have a year ago.

Outside, beyond the house, the city swelled and seethed.

*

In our country, when a girl marries, her parents present her with a partition screen, a jaali. The one at Mehmood Street spanned the women's quarters overlooking the garden; its carved lattice was decorated with geometric flowers and tiny egrets, their needle beaks etched into the wood. I watched the screen as the afternoon drew on, tracing it with my fingertips. The teak smelled dark and sweet in the rain. I had always thought that I would have a jaali of my own, in the Punjab, where my family have always lived.

Through the carved trellis, I could see the lawn at the back of the house. I was standing in the shadows, watching the water drip slowly from the leaves outside, when I sensed movement in the garden and Haamid, in dry clothes, crept across the grass. He lifted the latch of the gate and slipped out into the street.

Behind me, Joshna began to untie a new parcel of silk. She laid out the various threads, selecting colours for her hijab. Her eyes when she looked at me were kind. "Gold or green?" she asked and I went to sit opposite her. We unfurled a length of black silk out between us and began to embroider it from end to end, drawing the gold thread in and out to meet in the middle.

*

That evening, on the roof of the house, I stood by the parapet looking out over Lahore: at her terracotta domes, mosques, cinemas and temples glowing in the evening light. I did not hear Haamid as he joined me, but I felt him.

"Where have you been?"

"You know, Lakshmi," he said. I glanced at him as he came to stand beside me; I could see the Qur'an poking out of his leather satchel. "Go home," he said, finally.

"Haamid -"

"Please go home."

"I am home," I replied and I turned to him then. "Bahawalpur and Lahore are to be in Pakistan."

"You cannot go back to that school."

"I will be safe at Armitage. The teachers -"

"The English will leave."

"Not all of them," I said. "I live here, Haamid. I can finish my schooling here." In the silence that followed, we stared at one another.

He turned back to the city, but I felt his hand brush mine "They are talking about August the fifteenth," he said. "It is when the British will go."

"What else do the wise elders say?" I had thought my sarcasm would anger him and that he would leave, but that night he stayed still by my side, almost touching my hand.

"We're not children anymore," he murmured, his eyes moving over my lips, my cheeks, to the dot of red ash between my eyebrows. "Go home" he said, "Lakshmi please...you must leave Lahore."

For a moment, I felt him lean towards me in the darkness and I hoped that he would kiss me then, but he only left me alone on the rooftop where we used to meet, with the lights of Lahore shining into the distance.

Joshna was lying on her side when I entered our bedroom but she was not asleep. Through the walls I could hear the wireless in the women's quarters where Auntie Aisha sat up listening alone. I settled down next to Joshna, breathing in the scent of cardamom milk still warm in the air. Finally, as the notes of Lillibulero faded away on the BBC, together we strained to hear the voice of the broadcaster.

Soon afterwards Joshna and I returned to school.

*

One week before the fifteenth of August, Armitage College held a fire drill. Josh and I were asleep in our dorm when Miss Simmons woke us. She told us to wear our coats over our nightclothes and to put on our shoes. We were marched out, all 300 girls, lined up and led out into the darkness of the cricket pavilion. Our teachers followed, some with torches, some with guns. A homemade flag, found near the boundary of the school, was brought forward by one of the grounds staff - it was patched together from different shades of green and had a white crescent in the middle. I remember standing in the darkness, the leather of my shoes rough against my skin. Beyond the light of the torches the night pulsed, as bats circled overhead.

In the days that followed we were told to pack a small case of clothes and leave the remainder of our belongings in the boarding houses. At night, we bedded down on mattresses in the great hall, falling asleep to the whirring of the ceiling fans. Most lessons continued, however instead of sports we were restricted to walking in the gardens. I could see the grounds staff in their navy jackets, watching us from the trees.

When the fifteenth passed peacefully, a rumour began that we would soon be allowed back to our dormitories. Joshna and I were in the library one morning when I realised that the bells for assembly were not ringing. I walked to the glass doors overlooking the cloisters and saw one of the grounds staff in the courtyard below. He was dragging a girl by her plaits across the paving stones, she had a cloth wrapped around her mouth but I knew her, Samarthi, she sat next to me in Maths class. She was Sikh. Sam fought him, her shoes slipping on the floor of the cloisters. Another man in a plain kurta followed. He was dragging a second girl by her collar. I did not know her, but the ash on her forehead shone red as the man pulled back her head and slid the knife, long and heavy, into her throat.

I stumbled backwards. Joshna must have come up behind me for I felt her hand on my mouth, stifling my scream. She drew me through the library and down the back stairs. Our boarding house was deserted as we ran through the corridors. Together, we paused by the door to a linen closet. Joshna looked at my face and pushed me inside and all the lights went out.

*

The blood pounded in my ears as wisps of screams began to filter through the wood. They grew louder and louder as Joshna opened the closet once more. She was holding a hijab in her hands, the one we had made together.

"Put this on." I stared at her, silent and stupid, as she joined me in the linen closet. She looked into my eyes and wrapped the material deftly around my head, fastening it over my nose and mouth. Then she leaned forward and picked at the faint circle on my forehead, brushing away the last of the red powder with the pad of her thumb.

"Lakshmi," she said, stepping away from me. "We have to go."

"Where?" I asked.

"The track leading into the village."

"Across the cricket pavilion?" I took a breath; I was struggling to come out of my panic.

"We can hide in the trees until Haamid can come for us."

"Haamid knows about this?"

Joshna looked at me, all certainty gone. "He said he would come if he heard anything." She shrugged and I pulled her towards me; I could feel her shaking through the folds in our clothes. We stood for a moment, still together. Around us, through the wood and the walls, we could hear the screams. Finally, we pushed open the door and as the morning air rushed in to greet us so did the fear. "Run," Joshna whispered.

She took off ahead of me, down the servant's stairs and outside around the buildings. I was gasping as I ran out in full view of the school. The material of the hijab filled my mouth as I gulped at the air. We were nearing the dirt road when I heard shouts behind us. Groundsmen were walking through the flower beds leading to the chapel. Joshna screamed my name as she ran across the grass. I could see a truck on the edge of the cricket pavilion and inside, Haamid, shouting at me. I turned back to look at our school as the first wisps of smoke curled around the terracotta bell tower. Joshna grabbed my arm and pulled me into the cab. I was still staring at Armitage as Haamid put the truck into gear and we sped up the road.

*

People streamed in front of us as we drove out into the desert; assembly lines of families with their pans and their cattle. The truck veered to the left as Haamid swerved to avoid a group armed with shovels and clubs. "Get on the floor!" he shouted and Joshna and I fell together as the truck picked up speed. I was still holding her, crouched on the floor of the cab, when I realised Haamid was speaking to me.

"Laks," he said "I will take you to Khanqah Dogran, but I have to leave you there." His eyes were focused on the road. "The train should take you over the hills to Hoshiarpur." Haamid blared the horn as more people tried to approach the truck. "Lakshmi, are you listening to me? Do not go near the border towns, if your train is stopped, climb out."

"Have you heard from my parents?"

"There was no word at the house," he said and he did meet my eyes then. "There will be camps over the border. Write to us from there." I

57

looked at his face, at the hope and the doubt that I saw there. I felt him push a cloth parcel into my lap: Nestlé bars, his penknife, a water canister, money.

"I will wait to see if the train is in danger," Haamid said. "If it is safe, I want you to get out of the truck and run as fast as you can." Beside me, Joshna's grip on my arms tightened.

*

"Lakshmi, go on." I looked up to see the great steamer belching black against the sand. Haamid reached out and touched my cheek. I felt his fingers through the fabric of the hijab. "Go," he said gently.

Joshna was sobbing, her tears mixing with mine on my face. I hugged her close, feeling her body still round and plump with adolescence. I would never know her as a woman, I thought, as I pushed open the door and ran for the train.

"*Guard us with Your Hands. Destroy my enemies.*" The bani filled my ears as I stumbled into the carriage. The woman singing had gathered a crowd around her; they were praying in the language of the Punjab, the language of my childhood.

I listened to the words and recognised the thoughts behind them. They were praying that we would get across the border, that the train would not be stopped. We had heard stories, even at Armitage, of men wearing belts filled with cartridges. Carriages abandoned in the desert, alone but for the buzzing of the flies.

People hissed as I moved down the carriage, staring at Joshna's hijab wrapped around my face. I pushed through them and found a crate near a window. Behind me, people swarmed onto the platform, climbing onto the roof of the train. I leant my head back and watched as a foot, blackened with dirt, swung back and forth before the glass.

Haamid had put me on a rural track, avoiding the larger stations where riots would be waging. I stared out across the yellow scrubland, white in the midday sun, searching for the border. Slowly, we began to climb, wheels flying over wooden slats and rusted rails. Someone opened the window and there was the screech of metal as baked earth flooded the carriage. We had left everything, even our shrines, but the land remained.

We passed through settlement after settlement, each village

abandoned, small towns where refugees gathered, hoping to join those on the roof of the train. People grew quiet as we travelled; even the children were silent as they sat on their parent's laps or in the luggage racks above us. I looked into the distance and thought of my family. I wondered if they too were on a train headed to an India none of us knew.

I was peering into the desert when I saw the blue tints of spires on the horizon, the outline of a dome. As a town emerged out of the haze, I saw the glint of rifles on the line, figures of men. Others began to notice too. They struggled to stand from their positions, squashing toes, knees, climbing onto their fellows to get a view. Tendrils of fear, acrid and sweet, began to permeate the carriage.

As the train slowed, I put my hands to Joshna's hijab where it brushed against my face; we had not yet crossed the border and I did not know to which side the men might belong. Shoving at those around me, I unfastened the clasps which held the veil in place and whipped it over my head. For a moment, I held the damp silk between my fingers, looking at the spirals of gold thread along the edge, the embroidery we had done that day, Joshna and I.

Amidst rising shouts, I pushed my way through the crowd of bodies, climbing onto a seat by the window. The wind was hot on my face as I shoved at the glass. The desert flowed out all around me, rolling between India and Pakistan. I did not look at the soldiers on the line or the group moving toward us. I threw the hijab high into the air and watched as it caught and unfurled on the breeze, glowing against the light of the sun.

Jean Ashbury

Author of Lemonade with Ice

Jean Ashbury comes from Trinidad and Tobago. She is a teacher, traveller and writer. She is currently working on a collection of stories based on slavery and indentureship.

Lemonade with Ice

Andromeda, Perseus, are you there? Dad told me you would be twinkling in the sky long after we humans were dead and gone. I'm here by the window. Can you see me? Can you see my Dad, and Abbas, and Bibi?

I shouldn't be sitting here. Twice Mum said, Don't sit by the window.

The second time she said it so loud you'd think I was deaf. I can't move yet because I'm drawing a picture of tonight for my Dad and I must make everything look just like it is.

When Dad comes home, I want to show him where we've been and what we've been doing so I draw pictures every day. Things like the cake with ten candles Mum made for my last birthday and the pot of bubbles Shahnaz gave me as a present.

I've been drawing pictures for my Dad for about four years. Mum says I should stop because we don't have room for all my pictures. She calls them doodles and complains they're taking over the flat. I told Mum that when, if, we have to leave here, I'm taking my pictures. My clothes and everything else can stay behind.

I started drawing because of Mrs. Richards, my Special Education teacher. I was seven when I started school in London and I wouldn't speak to anyone. Some people said I wasn't right in the head so my teacher sent me to Mrs. Richards. I wasn't the only one who went to her class.

There was Sam from Sri Lanka who was always sniffing like he had a permanent cold. And Femi from Somalia who asked me time and again, Which tribe you belong? because of the scar on my cheek. And Benny from the flats in the tower block near school, who kept saying, What is two and two? Five! And Li from Taiwan who ran around the room saying, Fuck-fuck-fuck, the only words she knew.

On my first day, we sat in the teddy bears' corner and Mrs. Richards read us a story about a tiger who came to tea. I thought that was silly because that's not what tigers do, but I liked listening to her voice. Afterwards she asked me to tell everyone about myself and where I came from. I didn't speak so she told me to write about it. She couldn't read my language so she said, Draw something.

I drew tanks and soldiers shooting guns and smashed up houses and fire falling from the sky. Mrs. Richards stared at my picture for a long time, and she had that frown Mum gets between her eyes when Shahnaz refuses to wear her hijab.

You have quite an imagination, she said and put my picture in a drawer.

The next day I drew myself with a happy face, skipping in the park with friends. Mrs. Richards smiled and pinned my picture on the wall. After that, I drew happy pictures every day. Mrs. Richards would ask me questions like Mummy? Sister? If I nodded she wrote it on the back with the date. When the Head came to see what was going on, she showed him my drawings and said, We're making progress.

I started talking when I was with Mrs. Richards. I pretended to be her and I'd say things I heard her say. Like, Blow your nose Sam. Benny, two and two makes four. And, Stop swearing Li. It's not nice.

A whole year passed. A lady in a black suit came to see me. She listened to me read, made me do a lot of puzzles and asked Mrs. Richards if I was socialising. Mrs. Richards must have said, Yes, because they sent me back to normal class. After that I saw Mrs. Richards only in the playground. Sometimes she would tell people off for calling me Frankenstein.

I can't draw properly tonight. The charcoal keeps breaking because I'm wearing woolly gloves. I know Dad will say that's no excuse. He'll tell me that Michelangelo stood on a ladder for years with his head cricked back painting the Sistine ceiling, and I'll say, Dad, I know that already, my teacher told me. And he'll laugh and say, Who is this teacher? Take me to her.

Yasmin, have you taken your pills? Mum asks.

It's noisy tonight. I pretend not to hear.

YASMIN.

In a minute, Mum.

Naz, see she takes the pills.

Quick as a flash Naz is on my case. She stands in front of me with two white pills in her palm.

Mum says stop doodling and take these now, she says.

Naz is four years older than me and she thinks she's the boss.

I put the pills in my mouth and she gives me lemonade to wash them down. Not Mum's lemonade made from real lemons, but supermarket stuff that leaves a sickly-sweet taste on my tongue.

Open, Naz says.

I pretend I'm a goldfish…open, close, open. Naz peers into my mouth to see if I've swallowed the pills. When Mum does it, she pokes around my cheeks and under my tongue with her finger, but Naz is scared I'll bite her. When she goes to the kitchen, I take the pills out of my mouth and put them in my coat pocket. I feel a bit guilty. Tonight of all nights, I know I should take my medicine.

My feet are tucked up under me. I pull my coat and wrap it round tight. I love my coat. I wear it all the time, sometimes even in bed. It's a big, grey thing like an elephant. It flaps round my ankles and trips me up when I'm running, and the sleeves hang down to my fingertips and get in my dinner. Sometimes I pull the collar up past my ears and hide up to my eyes, but the wool hurts my scar. I think there's still some glass left in my cheek.

My coat looks like a Russian army greatcoat with five silver buttons across the chest. There used to be six but Betsy Parsons ripped one off when we were fighting.

Mum bought my coat for two pounds in a jumble sale. She scrubbed it with soap and sprayed it with deodorant. It still smells of somebody's sweat but now it's mixed with cumin and coriander from Mum's cooking which is why they call me Smelly Paki at school. I don't mind the sweat smell. It makes me think the last owner could have been the warrior princess Dad used to tell me about. She used to ride around the Steppes of Asia like Genghis Khan conquering her enemies. She didn't need pills.

And I didn't need them the day I beat up Betsy Parsons.

I was walking to class holding my hands inside my sleeves like a Victorian miss wearing a muff. Betsy and her friends were dotted round the classroom door like landmines.

Oh look, here comes the Paki, Betsy shouted.

She'd been calling me Paki since I started high school.

My knees wobbled and my feet slid as if the corridor had been greased. Betsy and her friends surrounded me.

Good morning, Yasmin, said Betsy, and her eyes locked on me like heat-seeking missiles.

I put my head down and tried to barge through. She put her hand out to stop me.

Don't they teach manners where you come from Paki? she asked. Say, Good. Morning. Betsy.

Her friends spat and shouted, Stinking wog. *Say, Good. Morning. Betsy.*

They started pulling my coat and pushing and shoving me. I fell. Betsy put her dirty Nike trainer foot on my cheek, the one with the scar and the glass. A million dogs started to bark.

I don't know how it happened but suddenly I was sitting on Betsy's chest and I was hitting her and hitting her and she was trying to throw me off but I had her pinned. I could see her eyes. They were big and scared and she was crying, Jeeesus, help, help. But everyone was screaming, Fight, fight, fight. And while I was hitting her, I felt as if I was galloping on a white horse, hair flying in the wind, charging enemy hordes and knocking them down.

Our Headteacher dragged me off. He suspended me from school that day. He said I should know fighting didn't solve problems. He didn't know I was a warrior princess, but Betsy knew. She doesn't mess with me anymore.

Crack. Crack. Crack. The racket outside is getting louder. It makes me wheeze. I puff on my inhaler and play with the pills in my pocket. I don't want to take them because I'm getting ready for another fight. Insha'Allah.

It's a witchy November night on Edgware Road. Fuzzy charcoal sky, ghosty pointy skeleton trees, black house shapes with yellow windows, and car shapes, dog shapes, and people shapes. I wish I could draw smell and noise but I don't think even Michelangelo could do that. I'll just have to write a description on the back as Mrs. Richards used to do.

I'm drawing as fast as I can. I hope I'll have time to finish. Not like last year (and the year before, and the year before) when I was A Major Concern and Mum had to call 999. Naz told me later that I had the biggest fit ever and the paramedics had to shock my heart lots of times to bring me back.

I'm cold, cold, cold. I'm wearing my coat, gloves and thick socks but my bones feel like they've been in the freezer. They've felt like this ever since we came to live here, our fourth home. Mum says I shouldn't complain because the people smugglers could have left us in Russia. That's why Sri Lankan Sniffy Sam used to say Tak, Tak—Danish for Thank you—because he and his parents ended up in Denmark. They thought they were coming to England. And because they didn't have any more money, they had to stay in Denmark till they got jobs and proper papers to travel.

I looked Russia up on the net and saw all the ice and snow. I'm glad we didn't end up there. I also read about a place there called Siberia where lots of people used to be banished. I wonder if the people smugglers left Dad in Siberia, and if he has a big furry coat and boots to keep him warm.

Shsssssss. A flame with a tail shoots across the sky like a comet. Another one follows. And another. My heart gallops like when Betsy chased me.

Clinks and rattles are coming from the kitchen. Mum and Naz are washing up…well, Mum is washing and Naz is drying. Mum doesn't let us wash up. She says we waste hot water and washing up liquid and she can't afford to give drain germs bubble baths.

I hear them laugh. Then I hear them humming a song, the one that makes me feel like I'm dancing through long grass and sand dunes out towards the blue sea with the sun shining on it like golden dinars. That would make a good picture if only I knew how to draw the sound of laughing and humming.

Mum's a little happy today. This morning the Home Office said we can stay in England for the rest of our lives. We've been waiting to hear that forever. It took a long time because we lost our papers.

As Mum is in a good mood I wonder if...

Mu-um, can we have the heating on? I ask.

Eating or heating, she says as always. I'll bring you a hot water bottle in a minute.

Naz calls our flat Hot Water Bottle Central because we have so many. Mum and Naz have one each, I have two, one for my feet, one for my hands. We don't have enough money to have heating for more than a couple of hours each day. Mum cleans offices every morning before we get up, then comes back before we go to school, then goes to work at the launderette down our street. Naz and I would like to do paper rounds to help out but Mum won't hear of it. She says it's not in our culture and Dad would be upset if he heard we were running around on the street by ourselves.

No, you have to say it like this, Naz says.

She's helping Mum to practise for her English speaking test. Mum is a dentist but she has to pass an exam in English before she can pull people's teeth out. She's failed three times. She says English is too hard and in any case at her age she shouldn't have to be a student again. Then she cries and I know she's not crying about English grammar but because she misses Dad and Abbas and she wants to go home and drink lemonade with ice.

No, I'm not going to speak about that. They can ask me anything, but I won't talk about that again. Mum is shouting.

In the test, she has to talk about home and family and our country. She's told so many people about these things, hung her head and sobbed in front of men in uniforms who didn't believe her, in front of women with clipboards, in front of lawyers with briefcases, doctors with notebooks, teachers with forms...

You OK, baby? Mum asks.

She stands beside me with a hot water bottle. Her eyes are red and she wipes her nose with the back of her hand. She looks through my drawing book.

I need a doodle. I'm writing to Geneva tomorrow, she says.

There must be a big file in Red Cross Headquarters with Mum's letters, copies of the last photo of us together and some of my drawings. We get letters back from the Red Cross saying they're doing their best. They've been saying that for years. I wish we could pin everything to the tree outside with a message saying, URGENT. *If you see this man, and this boy and this doll, please call Mrs. Habibi and her daughters on…*

Mum looks at my last drawing of Dad. She traces his hair, his eyes, his brow, his lips, and the two lines down the sides of his mouth.

You made him too grey, she says.

She turns the page to Abbas, my twin. She smiles and says, I could never tell you apart, except for…you know…down there.

Then she sees Bibi with her plaits undone, a hole where one brown button eye should be and her panties missing, and she breaks down.

Eventually she says, I'll put the fire on for a little bit, baby.

I like to toast my back when the fire is on. I always sit too close and my sweater scorches. That smoky smell always reminds me of Tent City. There were hundreds of tents and millions of people like us. I was three when we went there, Mum tells me. And I had three birthdays there, freezing at night, roasting in the day, hungry all the time.

Dad was always asking the people with the world on their tee-shirts when we could go to England, or America. Mum was always counting the days till the next food box arrived, and Naz was always complaining about going to the food tent for bread because she didn't like how the men looked at her.

Abbas wanted a big box of halva, and I wanted to sleep in my bedroom with the pink net and fairy lights over the bed.

There was a school in one of the tents. We went a few times but the teachers were strict and Abbas was scared of them. One day one of the teachers shouted at Abbas and he wet himself so Mum stopped sending us. A lot of the other children didn't go either. We spent our days playing hide and seek between the heaps of truck tyres piled by the wire fence.

When it was cold, men burned the tyres. It always took ages for the rubber to catch light and there'd be black smoke everywhere. Sometimes they burned the tyres even on hot days and ran around shouting and punching the air. Dad called it Demonstrating-for-Human-Rights and he would join in. Afterwards he would come home covered in blood and bruises and Mum would say, How long do we have to stay in this Hell-on-Earth?

One day Naz came back with her hijab off, her shirt ripped and her arms scratched. She cried for a week. Mum and Dad whispered a lot after that. Then one night, Dad covered us up in the back of a truck and told us we were going to Istanbul. He and Abbas and some men were in the back of another truck. Abbas started crying.

Shoosh, keep quiet, everybody said.

Abbas didn't want to leave Mum so I left my doll Bibi with him. I kissed Bibi and told her to look after him.

It was a long ride, and very bumpy like we were driving over big rocks. When the sun came up, we were in the mountains somewhere and Dad's truck was missing.

Mum said to the driver, Wait.

But he said we had to hurry to meet the lorry taking us to the boat. He said Dad would catch us up.

It's now four years and Dad hasn't caught us up yet.

Mrs. Richards told me a story once about Theseus the Greek man who went to kill a monster living under the ground. Theseus was afraid he would get lost in the tunnels but Ariadne, a kind lady, gave him a ball of string to help him get out. I wonder if there's a lady with a ball of string who will help Dad find us. Naz says I shouldn't say things like that because Mum will be upset to hear about another lady with Dad. Naz knows about stuff like that because she's got a boyfriend, Deepak the greengrocer's son, and she gives me hate looks when I smile at him.

The pops and bangs below my window sound like giant crackers. My insides jump to my throat and stick there.

Come away from the window, Yasmin, Naz says and starts pulling me.

Leave me alone. I have to finish my picture.

She touches the scar on my cheek to remind me I should know not to sit near windows, but I stay put waiting for the moon to come out.

There's smoke outside now. White smoke.

Bang. Crack. Crack. I get the shakes and I feel whoozy. That means the djinn that lives in my head is waking up and getting ready to knock me out. My djinn sits like a cobra on my brain, and strikes when she hears noises that sound like bombs going off and jets flying past. Post-traumatic stress disorder, the doctor called her, and prescribed pills to make her sleepy. I feel the ones in my pocket. Still a little sticky from my spit.

Below my window, streetlight shines on parked cars, not burnt out skeletons but whole new ones. Deepak is leaning against his father's van, smoking a cigarette. He's waiting to catch a glimpse of Naz. Two children go past him. It's Bonfire Night and they're pushing Guy in a pram. They're not afraid that a sniper will get them, or that a tank will rumble round the corner and run them over.

The moon comes out like a piece of butter from behind grey clouds and disappears again. Dad told me that when the moon saw bad things, it hides behind the clouds and cries and all its tears fall into space. I suppose that's why the moon is dry.

Crack. Crack. Crack. The noise sounds as if it's in the room with me. My head begins to spin but I can hear Mum saying, Shahnaz, close the curtains. Quick.

Naz grabs the curtain and pulls. She used to do that every night. Abbas and I would stop colouring and creep under the blackout drapes to watch the fireworks. One night a bang like the end of the world shattered the window. Good thing Dad is a doctor. It took him all night to take glass out of Abbas and me.

We're going on holiday Dad said after that. It was a funny kind of holiday. We didn't take the car, or suitcases, or our snorkels. Only what you can carry, Dad said.

Naz put on her red, heart-shaped sunglasses and her silver fairy dress. Abbas took his bird kite, his Eagle. I had Bibi, and Mum and Dad stuffed things under their coats till they looked like the tyre man in the garage sign. Dad put me on his shoulders, Mum carried Abbas and we went into the night.

Shsssssssss. Squibs chase each other in the sky and fizzle. Through a gap in the curtains I see sparks showering the houses. I'm trembling hard enough to fall over. I push my hands in my pockets, dig my nails into my palms and let the pain in my hand fight the one in my head.

Crack. Crack. Crack-crack. Rockets are going off everywhere. Light blinds me. My arms and legs dance like I'm having electric shocks. I'm on the floor telling myself I won't pass out, I won't pass out, I won't…

My cheek burns. The carpet smells of pee. I see feet with chipped red nails. Someone holds me. Another wipes my face with a damp cloth. I hear them speak.

I gave her the pills, Mum. Honestly.

I know you did, darling.

Shall I call 999?

No, I think she's coming round.

Someone is rocking me. I see a face, hair all tangled, eyes all sunken, lips all chewed.

Mum?

You're safe, baby.

Mum's warm, wet cheek touches mine.

I didn't pass out. I didn't.

No, you didn't. You won, my darling.

My djinn will return for a re-match, but for now, I am a warrior princess stinking of vomit and shit. Andromeda, Perseus, if you're watching, don't tell Dad you've seen me like this. Mum will clean me up soon.

You OK now, baby?

Mum, can we make lemonade?

Lemonade, baby? Tonight? But I don't have any lemons.

Naz can get some. Hassan is still open.

It's too late now, baby. We'll do it tomorrow.

You promise.

I promise.

Mum and Naz half carry me to the bathroom. Mum washes me as if I were a baby. She tucks me up in bed and whispers a song from our once upon a time life, and I remember the way we were before the desert storm came.

Lemonade with ice

*

There's a tree with shiny green leaves. Abbas and I are underneath with a basket. Dad shakes the branches. Lemons fall and lie on the grass like yellow goose eggs. Abbas and I pick them up. We load the basket, hold the handle together and stagger into the kitchen.

Mum peels the lemons and pours boiling water over the peel.

To get the essence to make the juice more lemony, she says.

Dad cuts the lemons in half and squeezes with his bare hands. It looks like he's pressing juice from the sun.

Naz says, Why don't you use the juicer, Dad?

And he says, A little effort makes everything sweeter.

And while Abbas and I kneel on chairs waiting with mint and sugar and ice cubes to put in the jug, Dad tells us about the stars. His fingers stab at the sky. Lemon juice drips down his arms.

Mum laughs and says, Hurry up Yusuf, we want to drink this lemonade today not next week.

When the juice is ready, we sit in the garden by a wooden table under a big white umbrella. Mum fills our glasses (even Bibi gets one) and we wait for Dad to take the first taste. He picks up his glass, holds it up to his nose and breathes in deep. Then he takes a mouthful of lemonade, swirls it round his mouth and swallows, slowly.

Miriam you've excelled yourself again, he says.

Mum looks at him from under her lashes and smiles.

Oh Yusuf, she says.

Naz picks out all the pistachios from the lokum and keeps them for herself.

Abbas flies his Eagle and gets it messed up in the lemon tree.

And I sit on Dad's lap, with Bibi, tasting sharp-sweet lemonade that is so cold my teeth tingle.

Sabo Kpade

Author of Chibok

Sabo Kpade's stories have been published in Verdad, Glasschord, Gertrude Press, The Write Room, and Sable. He is the lead critic for Royal African Society's whatsonafria.org and Media Diversified. His first play Have Mercy on Liverpool Street was staged by Talawa Theatre Company in 2014 and was longlisted for the Alfred Fagon Award in the same year.

His second play The Good General was a finalist for the Beeta Playwriting Competition 2015. After completing his first novel Anyone's Ghost, he is currently at work on a new play A Leg To Stand On. He lives in London.

Twitter: @sabo_kpade

Chibok

Maman Paulina hates me.

She hates that I am alive.

I know that if it came down to it, if the men had asked her to decide if to take me or her daughter, it wouldn't have been a hard choice. My mother wanted me to go and see her the day after I got home.

I told her that I didn't want to see anyone but she insisted that I had to so we didn't look unsympathetic. I never liked it when my mother did this – care too much what people might say.

"Tie your head tie properly like a child who has a mother,"

"When you're a given food in someone's home, never finish it so they don't think we don't have food in our house,"

"If you don't learn how to cook properly no man will marry you,"

and the one that always confused me was

"Even if it is a polytechnic you go to, do it, if not you will end up like me."

"Like how?" I asked her and she said "ask me, ask me as if you're blind."

I would have gone to visit Maman Paulina anyway.

I would have even lived in her house for days if it would help console her.

I would do more even though she never really liked me because she thought I was the reason Paulina refused to accompany her to hawk the corn she cooked outside their house. This used to cause arguments between her and my mother who believed me when I told her all of that was Paulina's doing.

She told me that her mother said I was a bad influence on her because I tied my head tie like a prostitute.

When my mother heard this she banned me from ever going back to Paulina's house.

Now she wants me to go and visit her. And while there I should show sympathy – cry if have to.

"But I already feel sorry for her and what if my tears don't come out?" I said to her.

"Make them" said my mother "or else you will look heartless."

I had no problem with going to Paulina's house. Partly because I got to escape the many people that came to visit me, if only to see what was so special about me that made God bring me to safety. People who never paid any serious attention to me now stared with pity.

People I had never spoken to now wanted to shake my hand and pat me on the head like some miracle child. If three wise men had showed up with gold bangles and earrings I wouldn't have been surprised.

My mother's friends who were all members of our church's zumuntan mata came as a delegation. One prayer by their leader, a woman we called Magajiya, was not enough. When she was done another member began another prayer. And after her, and at random, others also prayed as if to outbid each other in earnestness and thanks.

Mun gode Allah, allah

Mun gode Allah, allah Sarki

I wanted them all to leave so I could sleep, exhausted from trekking through the forest all night. My feet were swollen and blistered which made standing feel like a punishment. The hot compress and Robb with which my mother massaged my feet didn't reduce the swelling or the pain. Hungry as I was I couldn't keep solid food down. Minutes after I ate it all came rushing out so now my mother keeps a bowl beside me just in case.

Liquids I could handle. Zobo now tasted like chewing Panadol. But kunu I could stomach especially the way my mother made it with a little too much ginger. Paulina once drank it in my mother's presence but complained behind her back that it set her mouth on fire. There wasn't enough plaster in the house for all the cuts on my arm and the sole of my feet. We were going to the clinic but first I have to visit Maman Paulina.

"She hasn't spoken a word since you were taken" said my mother "seeing you will give her hope that Paulina is still alive."

I saw Paulina just twice since she was married off to one of the fighters. She was one of the girls brought to watch the first time I was being flogged in the public square for refusing to marry the boy who chose me as his wife. In an outburst fuelled by fear and rage, I told him "do not come near me, touch me or even speak to me."

But if I gave him more trouble he would shoot me since I was an *arnia*. I had to bite him on the shoulder to get him off me. When he reported me I was taken to The Square and caned 40 times. He did the caning.

The second time I saw her she was a different person.

I told my mother I couldn't visit the house of every other girl that was taken. She said it was just Paulina's because she was my best friend so my presence will give them hope of one day seeing Paulina.

My mother already had a pick-up truck waiting in the veranda. It belongs to Baban Melchizedek who delivers firewood to our compound. I always knew Melchi liked me because he would give us a little more wood than we paid for and would then ask me how school was going, what my favourite subjects were and what I wanted to be when I grew up.

I always told him to mind his own business because I was the one in SS1 while he follows his father around selling firewood in a truck. So I am the one who should be asking him about his future ambition.

He would laugh as if I had just told the best joke he had ever heard and say to me "good answer". But when he came with his father or when my mother came out to help me take the firewood inside, he pretended as if he had never seen me in his life.

Today, Melchi is all business as he and my mother help me into the truck. He didn't hold my arm and waist strong enough so I don't think he's enjoying touching me.

My mother and Melchi loaded me into the cab like the heavy log of wood I had become. Three weeks ago she would have teased me saying one day soon Melchi and his father are going to come and "make enquiries about my availability."

She would have laughed at her own words.

But on this five-minute drive to Paulina's house, not a beep comes from her lips.

All she does is fit me under her arms and hold me so tight that even in the hot breeze I could smell the wood smoke in her clothes.

My mother left it till we were just outside the compound to tell me that Baban Paulina along with the other fathers in our ward whose children were taken formed a search team that went into Sambisa forest to look for us. So I should thank him very well. Also, that Maman Paulina has not said a word ever since.

"Nothing" I asked her.

"Not a single word" she said.

Not my mother. She was overwhelmed with joy.

Midway through a sentence she would start praying.

And midway through a prayer she would start singing,

only to stop half way through that to continue what she was saying at first.

Not once has she asked me what happened to me or the other girls when I was held captive. It was my uncle who asked me how I escaped.

My mother listened but didn't ask any questions.

She might be giving me time to recover first. But if my hunch is right, she didn't want to know of every pain I suffered.

Being able to hold me once again was all she needed, was all she was interested in.

At Paulina's house, Melchi and my mother helped me out of the cab and into the compound. There were fewer people here than there were in ours.

They all stopped whatever they were doing except for Paulina's little brothers who carried on playing collapse.

There is no way they don't know that Paulina is missing.

Baban Paulina stood up to receive us. He really did look like he had been foraging in the forest and hadn't found time to wash himself. His cream kaftan had brown stains all over it and his legs were coated in harmattan dust.

Chibok

He thanked me and my mother for coming, and thanked Melchi for giving us a lift after which my mother told him to wait outside.

He said he was sorry for what I had been through.

He said that God had a plan for my life to have engineered my escape.

He thanked me for being a good friend to Paulina and then asked if we would like a drink.

Paulina's mother did not once look at me or my mother. Neither did she respond to our greetings. My mother told them I got home at dawn. I hadn't slept and could hardly eat. But she wanted to make sure that we come and commiserate with them. And that just as God brought me back, he shall bring Paulina back. There was still no word from Maman Paulina but just as we were about to leave she said -

"Why didn't you bring her back?"

"Why didn't you bring your friend back?"

"I'm sorry" I said.

"She is your best friend. You should have taken her with you."

I hadn't planned to say anything. But I had to.

"She didn't want to come with me"

This made all their eyes flash wide.

"What do you mean?" asked my mother.

"When their trucks were full, me and Paulina were among those they asked to walk behind it. I told her we should run into the bushes. She said she was too scared, that we should keep walking or else we will get shot. I'm glad I listened to her because some of the girls tried to run away and were shot at. I don't know who they were and they never told us if they killed them. After they made us convert and began marrying us off to their fighters, I told her that now they will never release us so we should still try to run away. She still said no because if we get caught, they will kill us. So I decided to run away on my own. They caught me the first

77

time and flogged me forty times. Look..."

I unbuttoned my blouse and turned my back to them.

Maman Paulina stopped crying. It was my mother's first time seeing it.

She chewed her finger to stop herself from crying.

I haven't seen the blisters myself but sometimes when I stretch my skin breaks into a new wound.

That was a lie. I was flogged for trying to escape after I refused to sleep with the boy that called himself my husband. I mixed things up and I couldn't later admit that I did. They wouldn't know what to believe.

What I didn't tell them and never will is that I saw her one more time.

It was in the public square where I was flogged.

She was brought for another reason. The execution of two boys one of whom I learnt had refused to wear explosives.

On this day it was two boys who refused to follow them on missions, and another one who refused to wear explosives.

They made the newly captured ones do the killing to toughen us up, and discourage dissent. Paulina was one of those asked to slice their throats.

They lay the first boy's neck next to a small hole one of them was made to dig, and gave Paulina the knife. She didn't hesitate, cutting him only once as if it was a tuber of yam. I haven't seen her since then.

I can't say a word about it to anyone. Not even my mother.

2

I asked my mother not to tell anyone at the clinic that I was one of the girls that were taken. But she said everyone in our ward already knew and that was why we had so many visitors at our compound. She said there was no shame in it – that they all shared joy at my return. Also, it will mean we don't have to pay for treatment.

The nurse treated my wounds with iodine and gave me Panadol for the pain and Ibuprofen for the swelling. She then referred me to the teaching hospital in Maiduguri where I would also get a pregnancy test and psychological evaluation.

My mother said she knew another nurse who could help us if indeed I was pregnant. I told her any child in my belly is mine and I will keep it.

Now she thinks I really need the psychological evaluation. Yes, I have lost my mind. The part that until recently had seen bad things but not evil. The part that used to think a man who beat his wife or the new bride who maltreats the children of her husband's first wife is going straight to hell. Now I think they just might not get the best room in heaven because nothing compares to what I saw Paulina do in Sambisa. She is the one who has lost her mind.

I'll say it again, this child is mine. God might not have put it here himself but I dare him to take it away after what I have been through. If he will allow for me and the other girls to be taken away, raped, made to slaughter people like Christmas goats with no hope of ever seeing our families again then he couldn't possible have a say in what I do with the child.

"Think of the shame. You will be carrying the child of a killer, a despicable human being. No one will come near that child,"

"Then I'll leave Chibok and stay with our relatives in Maiduguri. No one will know where I am,"

"You will have to drop out of school and hawk to raise it. Better to completely erase the memory of what you have been through."

How is that possible when I keep thinking I will wake up in that tent and will hear the tarpaulin fluttering in the sandy morning breeze again.

Beside me will be the boy who said his name was Dahiru but I as his wife I should call him *mai gida*; a boy who told me that if his father can give his five-year-old sister for marriage then a twenty-year-old like me is old enough to start bearing children; a boy who told me I must renounce Jesus and accept Islam as my faith and that if I don't, he had no problem shooting me because I was an *arnia* and his religion gave him the right to take slaves.

A boy who told me that rather than cry and feel sorry for myself, I should embrace my new life because no one will come to get me.

A boy who told me I was no longer in Nigeria where women's rights were not respected but in the Islamic kingdom to play an important role in the jihad.

It's not as if he gave me a choice in the matter.

My mother told Melchi we now have to go to the teaching hospital in Maiduguri so he offered to drive us there.

She forced some money into his hand but he refused to take it.

He agreed to come back the next day to take us back to the clinic to collect our referral forms. He also insisted that we let him drive us all the way to Maiduguri because my swollen foot will worsen if I sit for hours in a bus.

This made me see him in a new light. Not as the good for nothing weed-smoker with no future ambition besides selling firewood. I wanted to see him again.

3

The swelling on my foot has gone down. But the welts on my back keep breaking and healing, breaking and healing. My back now aches from lying on the bed every day. The moment I could walk without a stick I insisted on taking the rams out to graze. My mother didn't like the idea but she also wanted me to resume living a normal life. My uncle and brothers were horrified so they instructed me never to leave the compound.

When they left for his farm, my mother allowed me to take them down the road to the incomplete primary school building that had been overrun by vegetation.

Time and again, I would see her come out of the compound to check if I was still there. Glad as I am to be home, being free is an empty feeling. Not worthless, just without any form or life.

Urging the rams back into the pen was what brought back hot flashes to the night we were herded away. We should have known the moment we noticed all our teachers had vanished. The gate man was the last to leave.

Nothing good will ever come to them, their children and their grandchildren. The same way they abandoned us is the same way someone else will abandon their children. God will make a different type of hell for them.

My mother brought me back to myself when she came to meet me outside the pen. I always knew she had something important to say when she loosened her wrapper and tied it again even when it didn't need an adjustment in the first place.

Apparently, a girl came to look for me while I was out. She said she was from ABTI University and that she came to offer me a scholarship – for free.

There are dreams you didn't know you had until they came through. This was one of them. But my mother, brothers and uncle were aghast that this woman would see nothing wrong in coming to ask me to return to school.

She was chased away and warned never to return or else she will be reported to the police as being an agent for Boko Haram.

"But it's ABTI," I said to my mother "American University of Nigeria."

As if she had never heard of it.

"Even the rich people we know can't get their children into the school".

She said "she would find something for me to do. I could learn to sow or start trading but never would she let me go to another school."

To be frank I wasn't thinking of joining another school but going to ABTI was God's way of making it up to me. None of my brothers or uncle said a word about it to me. They must have agreed that it wasn't worthy of mention.

She came back the next day, this woman my mother spoke of. But she wasn't at all what I expected. She was young, no more than 30 though she carried herself like a mother of three. Her name was Hannatu and she looked really sad. Not just meek the way you have to be around adults but sober as if she came bearing bad news. No wonder she was chased away on her first visit. Nothing about her said she worked in a school for all she held in her hands was an Olympic exercise book.

I expected my mother to be hostile. I waited for her to chase the lady away again. Instead she let Hannatu sit with us in the veranda and offered her *kunu* which she gladly accepted. Most visitors make a show of turning down any offer of food or drink to save face. And when they did say yes, they always left some in the plate or cup so as not to come across as gluttons.

"You came all the way from Mayo?" asked my mother.

"From Yola where I work in the university yes but my father is from Damboa."

"You're one of us so you know what our daughters have been through. Two hundred and nineteen parents are in anguish right now. So why did you come here to make it worse?"

And then she told her story. Her father was a police man in Maiduguri until he lost his eyes when Boko Haram bombed it to free their members who were held in the cell. He was one of the few who survived. Her sister Talatu was a JS1student in my school and was among the two hundred and nineteen that were taken. She said this with no feeling on her face, no visible sign that she had been affected by it. My mother's face soon glistened with tears. I didn't know her sister Talatu. JS 1 students were freshers and too far my juniors for me to have had interactions with her. I can't even recall her face but I'm sure I'll recognise her when I see her.

It shocked me when she said she had given up on ever seeing her sister but she wants to help those who escaped, to "bring meaning to their lives."

I told her not to give up. I was there at the camp. Just as I managed to get away, so will Paulina. This reduced her to tears and sobs. I made to console her but my mother held me back. She wanted her to cry it out – her pain, her misfortune, her bad luck – she wanted her to pour it all out. I think it did her some good.

Finished, she mopped her cheeks with her wrapper and told us what led her to our house. She had convinced the Director of Education in ABTI to help raise tuition fees for all 57 of us. So far, she and the DE as she then called him had managed to get enough for 10 students. I will be one of them if I just said yes. Imagine that, a scholarship to ABTI and all I had to do was say yes.

My mother thanked her sincerely, told her how sorry she was about her sister and promised to pray and fast for her return. But there was no way she would allow me to join another school because we have all been warned.

Hannatu explained that ABTI was a boarding school and the university is number one in Nigeria. My mother asked her how many girls had accepted her offer and she said just three. She read the names from her notebook. Hadasha Yohanna, Rebbeca Bitrus and Zuwaira Saminu. I know them all. Zuwaira is in SS2 and she is the school time keeper. Or rather was the school timekeeper. Hadasha and Rebbeca are in my year.

Hannatu said she had only been to the three wards in the local government and had seven more to go. She had hired a bike man to take her around and will not leave until the remaining 54 girls said yes.

She tore two sheets from her notebook, scribbled on them and squeezed each into my hands before leaving. My mother promised to speak to my uncle but assured her there was no way he would say yes. This alone made Hannatu happy enough to hug me and my mother as if we had just done her a huge favour. The whole thing was confusing.

My uncle said no of course. He even suggested that Hannatu might be an agent of Boko Haram sent to find every one of us that escaped. He asked me if I knew her sister Talatu who Hannatu said was taken. I told him that senior students don't interact with juniors.

He took this as proof that Hannatu was lying about the scholarships because there had been no mention of it by our councillor or chairman of the local government or the wife of the governor on any of their visits. So how could an unmarried woman from Damboa have enough money and influence to send fifty-seven girls to ABTI for free? A fee for one year alone is five thousand dollars.

My uncle promised to report her to soldiers, if she came back, and they were known for killing anybody accused of belonging to Boko Haram.

I decided to set the rams free. I can no longer stand dragging them to graze with a rope around their necks or force them into a small hut in the evening and lock them up. No one should be held captive against his or her will. They deserve to live freely and should fend for themselves the best way they know how.

My uncle will hate me for it. I know he's expecting a profit come Easter or Eid. He should know that the same way he plans to sell them at a good price is the same way Boko Haram were selling the girls as cheap brides and slaves along with using us as human shields. As long as they're

Sabo Kpade

not causing harm, everybody deserves to be free whether they be young girls, rams or a wooden stool if it is able to breathe. So I let them all out.

The next morning I hurried out to the pen. I wanted to be the one who discovered the rams had fled. That way I would not be suspected to have freed them. I needn't have bothered. Every single one of the rams came back. Some were in the pen and others lay outside it idly eating corn feed. They don't know any other home

I then went straight into my uncle's room and woke him up. I knelt down before him and begged him to let me go to ABTI. I told him that now, more than ever, I want to finish school. I appreciated how he had never treated me any different from his own children and for that I will forever be grateful. But I had to follow this path to wherever it will take me.

4

When Hannatu left for Yola, she had managed to convince nine of our parents to accept the scholarship. When she came back with a bus to take us, 20 of us were waiting for her. I thought she would be overjoyed but she was despondent. Seeing my school mates was the saddest reunion. There were no hugs, no joy at being the lucky ones to have escaped. We hardly spoke to each other. I for sure had little to say to any of them.

Hannatu said her school could only sponsor 10 girls but all their children are taken. Some begged. Others stood by and watched as the fate of their children were decided. She assured us that she had written to the governor and the presidency but they're yet to make their donations. But none of the parents would leave. I certainly wasn't going anywhere. Hannatu brought out a phone and shut herself in the bus.

As we waited, another girl, Saratu Bello, came running with her father. She was the one who we heard had been married off and was now in Kaduna with her husband.

It didn't look like she went anywhere or even had a change of clothes since the night we were taken. She wore the checkered pinafore we used as dorm wear in our old school.

When her father was told what the problem was he went mad. He raised his voice asking us all if what he was told was true. Most of us simply nodded.

84

Baban Saratu knocked on the door of the J5 asking to speak to Hannatu. She signalled for him to hold on for her to finish her call but he kept on knocking so she came out.

"You said you were going to take her. You begged me to let her go with you" he said.

"I also said I can only take ten" she said.

"Why ten? Take all of them"

"There isn't enough money"

"Who will you leave behind?"

She looked through her list then looked at us all.

"We don't have to go to ABTI," I said to her, "find us a cheaper school but take all of us."

"The school raised the money. They want to be responsible for you."

"You can't leave my daughter behind." said Baban Saratu "What if it was your sister? Would you like for her to be left behind?"

She shut herself up in the bus again and sat down with her face away from us. Baban Saratu turned to us his anger giving way to confusion.

"Her sister was also taken." I said, annoyed.

"Taken where?"

He looked from face to face but no one said a word. Slowly, it came to him just where her sister was taken to. You should have seen the shame on his face. He took off his hat and rubbed his head as if to dust off his insensitivity.

As I have come to realise, it wasn't just us girls that were traumatised; parents were also given to strange behaviour. If my uncle had been there he would have taken this as a sign that I was not meant to go to ABTI. He has never seen the point in a woman going to university only to end up a housewife. His faith was in handiwork – farming, baking, hairdressing and tailoring. It wasn't even his decision for me to go to Chibok Secondary School in the first place but my mother's.

"Why spend all that money on her when she will end up in her husband's house raising children?" he would say. But bless him, he left the decision to my mother and this one to me. In this way I am fortunate. It has brought me this far to the front of a J5 bus that will take me to my future. Or not.

When Hannatu came out of the bus she had pulled herself together. Baban Saratu looked sorry though he didn't say it. Hannatu cleared her throat and spoke up as if addressing a multitude.

"I have been told to only bring 10" she said raising her phone in the air as if to show just who it was she had been speaking to "and I have to do what I am told because I don't own the school, Atiku Abubakar does. But no one of you should be left behind. If we can't do anything about your 219 school mates that are in God-knows-where right now, we should do something about all twenty-one of you that are here today..."

"22," said Saratu Bello.

"Yes, 22. That leaves out 35 girls that I could not reach. I will keep searching for them. Nigeria must pay for what for how much it has failed you all."

"So I have decided that every one of you is coming with me. The Director of Education will not be pleased and God knows she has done her best. But if it means we all go to Atiku himself, if it means we knock on Governor Shettima's door, if it means we keep a vigil at Aso Rock we will so that everyone of you will get the education these evildoers do not want you to get. Now please form a single file and get on the bus. Lap each other if you have to but we all going to ABTI."

She beckoned us onto the bus and we climbed in, in a single, quiet file. From my aisle seat in the middle, I couldn't see my mother to wave her goodbye.

Tyler Keevil

Author of Cassandra to the Sea

Tyler Keevil grew up in Vancouver, Canada, and in his mid-twenties moved to Wales, where he now lives. He is the author of two award-winning novels, Fireball and The Drive, and his short fiction has appeared in a wide range of magazines and anthologies in Britain, Canada, and the U.S. His story collection, Burrard Inlet, was nominated for the Wales Book of the Year, the Edge Hill Story Prize, the Frank O'Connor Award, and the Rubery Book Award. One of the stories from the collection, 'Sealskin', was awarded the Writers' Trust of Canada / McClelland & Stewart Journey Prize. Among other things, Tyler has worked as a tree planter and ice barge deckhand, as well as in factories, restaurants, video stores, and shipyards; he is currently a Senior Lecturer in Creative Writing at the University of Gloucestershire.

Website: tylerkeevil.com

Cassandra to the Sea

On that last day my sister's skin was like crepe paper, dry and illuminate, glowing, as if some flame had started burning and was going to incinerate her from the inside out, unless I got her to the sea, where she was meant to be. She woke up in the room across the hall in the small mountain cottage where she had come to die and called my name. She called it in a whisper, but in the stillness of the place the whisper carried like a klaxon. I leapt up, ready, grabbed my shorts, hopping into them as I crossed the hall, thinking that she needed water, ice, fruit, codeine, morphine – any of the things that she needed and had been needing. I tripped as I entered her room (my legs got caught in my shorts) and I fell over with a sort of clownish elegance, flat out on my side, smacking the cold tiles. Cassandra started laughing, and her laughter ended in a terrible choking gag that blew a crimson bubble onto the pillowcase – a pillowcase that was now stained mottled brown from so many similar bubbles, blown over time, as she slow-burbled the life out of her lungs and chest and heart and soul, breathing it into the good night air of Sikinos.

I got up and went to her and dabbed the bright sticky bubble away with tissue, wiped her mouth and lips; she submitted to this with a resignation that had arisen from necessity, and familiarity. I asked her what she needed and she told me that it was time.

"Are you sure?" I asked.

"Have I ever said that before?"

"No."

"But you seem the same as yesterday."

"I need you to take me down there. I need you to do what you promised."

"Okay," I said, and didn't make a move to do anything.

"Okay?"

"Okay."

"It'll take me a few minutes to get things together."

"Be quick."

As she said it she coughed again and leaned over and blew more blood onto the floor. There was something painful and dramatic about it and I wondered if she'd triggered the cough on purpose to accentuate the severity of the situation and reinforce her belief that it was finally happening, after all these months. I daubed her mouth again and squeezed the bulb of morphine. It dangled above her bed and was attached to a transparent sack. There was something vaguely aquatic about it: the long tentacle that hung down and the kelp-like bulb that administered a dose. Like a one-armed octopus, hovering over her. As if one of her marine animals had followed her up from the shore to be near her, until she could return.

She smiled at me, her teeth laced with blood and rotten from all the bile, the acid. If somebody who'd known her in her prime – muscular and powerful, sleek as a shark as she sliced through the water – had seen her now, they would have been shocked, horrified, and might not even have recognized her. In part I knew that was why we were here, on some quasi-mythical island in the Aegean: so she could be away from all that and let them keep their memories of that other her. Only I was entrusted with this, and I had seen it happen slowly, over time, creeping upon her, as if each night some vulture was alighting on her and sucking her dry. The withering of muscle, the shrinking of skin to bone. My drying up, landlocked, skeletal sister. But her eyes were still hers. If anything they seemed even brighter, and were permanently moist, shining.

"Puck," she said, which was what she'd always called me, though really Bottom would have been more appropriate. "I was right to bring you. You were so strong for me."

The way she said that – as if she were already gone, speaking to me from the other side – struck me like a tuning fork. I felt the reverberations run through me, a seizure of frisson, and for the first time had an inkling that she was serious about this. And why wouldn't she be? She had always had that sense of timing and intuition. It was why she'd been so good with the sea – both in it and on it – and the animals that inhabited it. She was part animal herself and if there'd been a tidal wave coming she would have known, like the birds that flew to some far off mountain or the rodents that scurried to higher ground. And in a way I suppose there was a tidal wave coming to wash this all away, and her with it.

"I'll be right back," I said, and turned and ran into the wall.

*

Downstairs we had blankets, clothing, chains, weights, an anchor, a wheelchair, and a long white shroud that she'd bought in Marrakesh, in Jemaa El-Fnaa, when she'd known she was dying but still felt fine and had gone on an extravagant, romantic mission to find it. She had haggled with the draper, speaking in fluent, forceful French, regaling him with the full story of her life, and impending doom: a Greek tragedy in miniature. She told the draper about her early passion for marine biology, her research, her awards, her love of diving and her quest to save various species (including her campaign on behalf of the rare and underappreciated roughback batfish) that were threatened by whalers, by poachers, by pollution, by rising sea temperatures. She made it all sound as dramatic as it had been, leading up to her collapse at the lectern during a speech for Greenpeace in Waikiki.

At first, we all assumed it was due to exhaustion: me, her friends, her lover Henri, who had not been invited to Sikinos like me, or even told where she was going. Knowing Henri, he was currently scouring the Aegean, flying back and forth in his single-engine Cessna, dragging banners across the sky and dropping leaflets with her photo on them: have you seen this woman? He had said if she left without him he would never forgive her and then he'd broken down and kissed her hand and begged her forgiveness and said he would forgive her anything – even his own murder. Darling, she'd said. My darling Henri. He was her darling, I was her Puck. There were other players in her drama and we all came together to make up a wonderful cast, the *dramatis personae*, very aware that we were but bit players in a more important life and happy to support her.

But the collapse. She had been pushing herself so hard: the book, the lecture tour, the various dives and photoshoots. Exhaustion. It had to be exhaustion. They wanted her to go in for tests (just as a precaution) and she said she was too busy but we – all of us, but mostly Henri and myself – convinced her to submit, relent. Mostly because we felt it would give her a brief respite in the hospital while we awaited the results. And of course afterwards I felt, insanely, that we had all contributed somehow to

91

her demise. That if she hadn't actually had the tests she wouldn't actually have had the cancer. It was as if the acknowledgement of the possibility of her mortality actually made her mortal, when she had always seemed more like something else. A goddess who'd fallen out of Olympus, or an alien queen that had beamed down to earth, to illuminate us for a time with her passion, her fierceness, her benevolence.

She told all that to the draper in Marrakech and by the end of the tale other artisans and craftsmen had come into his souk to listen. Mint tea was brewed and shared. Silver Hands of Fatima were offered to her. Cooked meats and star-fruits were distributed: not the kind they sold to tourists but the ones they kept behind the counter, for friends and locals. And the draper, of course, had to give Sandy the shroud at a ridiculously low price. He did so with a kind of grudging respect, folding it easily, like a baker turning dough – impressed less by her tragic plight and more by the flare and panache with which she had shared it.

The shroud was a gift from one showman to another.

I removed the shroud from its trunk, carried it over to the stairs, and hung it from the bannister, like a Halloween ghost. Before fetching her I needed to get everything else ready. First I went out the door to the patio, bumping my head on the low stone arch. I had done this perhaps a hundred times in the months since we'd arrived. My scalp had all kinds of cuts, lumps, and abrasions on it. I had knocked one patch so many times that the hair had actually stopped growing: I'd somehow killed the follicles. And yet still I bumped it, again, in my hurry. I winced and rubbed the spot as I walked to the car – a beat-up Namco Pony that we'd bought upon arrival. There had been no rental companies on the island and so we'd had to barter for it at the local market in Alopronia. It looked like a giant red golf cart. I got in and started the engine, which turned over a few times before catching, coughing, sputtering to life. I backed the Pony up to the cottage steps and left it running.

Then, back inside to get the weights and chains and anchor. We had picked these up in the market, the same place we'd bought the car. The man had assumed the weights were for fishing and the chains and anchor for the small Greek *gaïta*, or fishing boat, which we had also bought, and we'd let him believe that and listened to his advice on their use and upkeep without letting on that they were all for Sandy's body, to keep it down.

I loaded those into the back of the Pony, which didn't have a trunk but rather a sort of open tub like the back of a Jeep. Under the weight the rear suspension sagged and the whole carriage dropped, riding low. That didn't worry me because we'd driven up there with that load so I saw no reason we wouldn't make it back down. Over the backseat, which was as hot and tacky as tar from being in the sun, I spread a thin wool blanket that our mother had knitted for Cassandra when she was very young. Cassandra had some vague memories of our parents but I didn't. It had only ever been her, for me. She'd been both sister and mother.

Into the glove compartment I tucked a bottle of water and a dozen strawberries, which were her favourite fruit and even though she could no longer keep anything down she liked to chew them and taste them and spit them out. She ate strawberries like you might eat sunflower seeds, or chewing tobacco: the gentle gnawing, the savouring, the thin line of spit, spattering into the dust. And I never knew if the red was just strawberry juice or also blood but that had stopped mattering, and bothering me, a long time ago.

Only when all that was ready did I return to the shroud and gathered it up. I did not know how you were supposed to hold a funeral shroud so I cradled it in front of me, draped over both my arms, like those fabrics the priests carry on the way to the altar. I felt very pious and devout as I marched up the stairs to where Cassandra was waiting. When I entered her room her eyes were closed and her body was utterly still, and I was so alarmed that I hit the doorknob with my elbow – right on the funny bone – and stepped on the portion of the shroud that was dangling in front of me, tripping again, this time falling forward onto the bed and throwing the shroud across her. She opened her eyes, shocked awake, and snorted at me.

"You were so still," I said.

"Oh, please."

"Okay, okay. I know."

I moved the shroud and folded back the covers on one side of the bed – leaving the other still covering her. I changed the sheets every day and also the sack that hung off her side into which all her fluids went. When I say fluids I am not trying to be polite: it was no longer urine or stool, piss and shit, which came out. Nothing was being ingested to warrant that. It was just liquids. Just a sort of water that had passed through her system, seeming to come out as clean as it went in, maybe cleaner. The water was drawn from a local well and was murky and brackish and we probably shouldn't have been drinking it, but of course for Cassandra it didn't matter.

I placed the shroud beside her and unfolded it. It was longer than a sleeping bag and twice as wide. It was made from fine-spun silk. It was like unfolding a cocoon still waiting for its occupant, for some creature about to reach imago. When it was all spread out like that – with a diamond shaped section at the top, which would form the hood or cowl – I removed the rest of the covers from Cassandra; she was dressed only in a shift and it had been a long time since I'd seen her body in full daylight. It was all gnarled like an effigy put together out of twigs and twine: the knobby joints wider than the limbs, the skin pale as birch-bark. A stick-woman figure.

At one time my sister could swim three Olympic lengths – 150 metres – on a single breath. I don't know what the world record is and she would have expressed only disdain about such statistics but I saw her do it on more than one occasion. And in the open water – where she was more at home and more in her element – she could go farther. While we were snorkelling, she often went so far and for so long that I sometimes wondered if she would ever come back. And in wondering I was only half-worried that she'd pushed herself past her limit, that her lungs had shut down or her heart had burst. Because part of me was more fearful that she'd simply grown gills and decided to leave dryland behind for good, and me with it. And I didn't know what would have been worse: to lose her or to be abandoned.

She was still so long of limb. The sickness hadn't taken that. Over six feet, with hands that lay curled at her sides, by her thighs, and wide feet that were flat bottomed and full, more like flippers than feet.

"What are you staring at?" she said tenderly.

"Sorry."

"You should be used to all of this by now."

"I'm never going to be used to this."

Cassandra to the Sea

I picked her up and shifted her onto the shroud. You hear the phrase 'like picking up a feather' but as a simile it is essentially meaningless. Many things are as light as feathers, or lighter. I would say her entire body was about as light as a large salmon. That was what it felt like: as if I'd landed some precious fish for a short time that now had to be thrown back. I removed the morphine drip, and began to wrap her up in the shroud, crossing one side over her body, and then the other, and then knotting the cowl beneath her chin. She gazed up at me from in there with wide and defiant eyes and asked me how she looked.

"Like a silkworm."

I knelt to lift her and as I did she curled towards me. On the way out the door I was paying so much attention to not bumping her head on the doorframe that I cracked her shin on the other side of it. It was those long legs of hers, sticking out. I had carried her before – up and down the stairs, to and from the toilet and patio – but I still hadn't gotten used to manoeuvring with her. The stairs were tricky as well, since they were narrow and bowed in the middle from years of use, and steep as a ladder. I had to hold her sideways and cross-step down precariously. This was not easy for somebody as clumsy as me. Sandy had always been the quintessence of elegance, both in and out of the water, and I was the opposite: I'd had more injuries, mishaps, and falls than a drunk acrobat. It was a real feat, getting down those stairs – and one of the only things I did right that day.

I stood for a moment at the bottom, adjusted my hold on her, and headed grandly towards the porch – cracking my head on the stone arch, for the worst and last time.

*

My plan was to lay her flat in the backseat but she instructed me, peevishly, that she wanted to be sitting upright, in the passenger seat, so that was where I put her. If she'd been able to drive she would have insisted on that, too.

I hustled back upstairs for the bag of morphine and the drip, and when I came down again she had flopped over onto her side across the driver's seat. I eased her upright and this time put the seatbelt on her to hold her there. After hanging the drip from the sun visor, and reinserting the needle into her cannula, I tucked one of those travel pillows – the kind shaped like a horseshoe, which people use on airplanes – behind her neck. It obscured her view somewhat but would at least prevent her neck from wobbling around. Then I got out the water bottle and poured some on a cloth and wetted her lips, which were parched and cracked and looked like wax paper. She'd been too long up that mountain, in the heat, away from water. I asked her if she was okay, which made her laugh. No blood this time. Sitting up seemed to help with that.

"Okay isn't quite the right word, Puck. But you're doing fine."

I put on her sunglasses and stayed kneeling by her for a minute, penitent.

"You need to drive me, now," she said.

"We're really going, aren't we?"

"I'm really going. You're just taking me there."

I sat down in the driver's seat and shut the door, which was big and heavy in the way the doors of old cars are. I eased off the emergency brake and soft-footed the gas pedal and we rattle-rolled over the driveway, gravel popping beneath the wheels. In the middle of the drive was a rock that was too big and embedded to move, and I slowed as we approached it. Even so, some part of the Pony's undercarriage rasped against it, which hadn't happened on the way in. That worried me, but not as much as it should have.

The driveway did not end but slowly transformed into a dirt track, which was the only route down the mountain. The cottage we'd rented was about a mile above Chora, a small town on the north coast of Sikinos. Sandy had chosen it because she felt she was less likely to be found hidden up in the hills, by Henri or anybody else, and because it was close enough to the sea that we could go down every day, until she became too weak to swim safely, and also because she had a special affection for the islanders, and the island – having fought to protect its fishing reef from the effects of tourist boats and ferries that had been destroying it slowly. They all adored her. They called her *erọméni̦ ti̦s thálassas*: the mistress of the sea.

The next cottage along was owned by a local couple who had an olive orchard. There were five of them – all lean and sun-browned, the children small and interchangeable. As we passed the father was standing in the orchard, inspecting or picking olives. He saw us and held up a hand. Sandy raised one arm in exchange, the shroud rippling a good foot behind her forearm. In her sunglasses and headscarf she looked like the skeleton of Grace Kelly, risen from the dead, bidding adieu to long-time fans.

Our neighbour, like all the islanders, knew why we were there. Whereas back home the idea she'd proposed was met with dismay, disbelief, shock, anger, on Sikinos it was merely accepted. We'd been treated politely and kindly. Gifts had been delivered to our door – homebrewed wine and pungent smelling goat's cheese wrapped in cloth and big jugs of pickled olives that had a tough skin and that we weren't sure whether we were supposed to eat raw or cook them as you might zucchini. Prayers had been offered. Nobody doubted the validity or questioned the sanity of somebody who'd opted to come out there to die in solitude. At first they had thought I was her husband until I explained a few times that I was her *adelfós,* her brother, and they had thought that perfectly understandable as well. Family is important to the Greeks and perhaps that was part of why we'd both always felt at home there, every time we'd visited.

Beyond the orchard I rounded a bend and saw the donkey cart coming up the track the opposite way. There was a passing spot near us but the cart – which was owned by an old man who lived high up in the hills, in a villa we'd never seen since it lay beyond our cottage – was moving in Mediterranean time. Slow, ponderous, gentle. This had suited us for many months but now I was in a rush to get Sandy down there, so she could die the way she wanted. Part of me still hoped or thought this was a false alarm, the start of many such trips – that she would be like the stoic Chief in Little Big Man, who continually believed it was his day to die and wandered up the mountain to do so, though we would be doing the opposite, going down, and spending the day at the beach before returning home, relieved and satisfied that it would not happen, at least for another day. But the part of me that was hoping for such an outcome was at odds with the part that was terrified this really was the day, and that, after all this waiting and all this planning, I would screw it up somehow, in the way I was prone to do. If Sandy had been at the wheel and able to drive there would have been no problems, but because it was me the chaos and potential for disaster had to be factored in.

The chance that something could and would go wrong. Murphy's Law squared. Puck's Law.

"Why have we stopped?" Sandy asked.

I hadn't realized that, behind her glasses, she had closed her eyes.

"There's that old man," I said. "Should I keep going? Make him move aside?"

"No," she murmured, twisting a wrist in a gesture of dismissal. "Let him pass."

I turned off the car and we sat there, with the Aegean sun pressing down on us, the sky that impossible azure blue, hot as neon and swirling with cloud, as the donkey came clopping towards us, its hooves tocking like a metronome, echoing amid the mountain quiet.

While we waited I told Cassandra a story, or remembered it for us, about the time we had been diving off the Great Barrier Reef and I'd nearly been swallowed by a whale shark that had been inhaling krill. The thing had carried me around, half inside its mouth, for maybe five minutes before Cassandra had managed to latch onto it and help extricate me. I told the story from my point of view, as I remembered it: peering deep into the dark belly of the beast, which was as confused and terrified as me, as it swam in circles and thrashed and shook and tried to spit me out. My oxygen tank was caught on on the shark's upper lip, near the snout. I don't think anybody has ever had so much time to consider the interior of a whale shark's mouth: a great toothless void. I was stuck there for so long that the initial panic had actually subsided and I was coming to terms with the possibility of my absurd death when Sandy had saved me.

Beside me in the car Sandy's silkworm shape was shaking, the laughter evident as little delicate tremors that coursed through her body. When I finished she managed to roll her head towards me and gazed at me with her Jackie Onassis glasses, and in that moment it looked as if those lenses really were her eyes – as if my sister had been transformed into some giant larvae.

"When we surfaced," she said, "you kept asking me if it had actually happened. You thought you were hallucinating or high or that you had died or that you were dreaming."

"And I didn't even get a damned photo."

"I did."

It had gone viral, that photo. This shot of me flailing helplessly in the mouth of a whale shark. She'd won a bunch of awards for it, too – and had wanted me to come to the ceremonies but I was too embarrassed. I asked her not to name me and I felt if I went I would have revealed myself as the clown. Most people probably figured it out, anyway. It was the kind of thing that would happen to me: getting stuck in the mouth of a whale shark.

"What did you think about, when you were in there?" she asked.

"You," I said.

*

The old man in the cart stopped as he pulled alongside us. He tipped his flatcap and grinned, showing his teeth, white as pearls hidden in the tanned satchel of his face. His donkey was sweating and caked in road dust but seemed content, happy to rest, flicking its tail back and forth at unseen flies. In the man's cart was a pile of shells and stones, taken from the shore. We had passed him many times on our trips to and from the sea and often wondered what he was doing, this man who took large portions of the shore up into the mountains. Sandy had come to the conclusion that he was building another beach up there, all to himself, which seemed as likely an explanation as any.

In the smiling silence the dust that the old man had been dragging behind him caught up and gave the air a diffuse, soft quality. He said something in Greek, and I caught the word *'thálassa'*. The sea. Yes, I replied, in my broken Greek. We were going to the sea.

'Asfalés taxídi, ereméni.'

It was only after he pulled away that I realized he might have asked if we were going not to the sea, but in the sea, or under it, and that seemed odd. It was as if he had guessed and understood that today was the day and had taken it in stride – merely wishing her luck on the voyage. As if it was a natural, everyday thing. And of course it was. It was.

"What are you waiting for?" Sandy whispered.

"Nothing," I said, and started the car.

There was a long stretch to the next passing spot and after the interlude with the donkey I didn't want to get stuck again. So maybe it was my fault, the way it happened. I was not speeding but I was going faster than I had before our break. Then there was the fact that the Pony was riding low and perhaps the tires were not flat but less inflated than they had been, months before, when we'd first come up to the cottage. We only used the car for our short trips to the beach so I hadn't thought to check the tire pressure. It had never seemed to matter. And of course we hadn't been using the car at all lately, so there was that, too.

Around the next bend were several rocks that had probably fallen off the hillside to the right. I didn't have time to stop. I should have swerved but I froze and did not think of that, not until we were upon them, and by then it was too late. I felt the lurch and heard the grinding shriek of the undercarriage, and then there was a terrible clamouring from beneath us. I didn't stop. I felt that if I stopped the truth of what had happened would be made real and that if I kept going, with my foot on the gas, we might get down to the bottom of the hill and beach, like you see in films when people ride out a flat by driving on the rims. But that didn't happen: the car shuddered and bucked and the engine died and we ground to a halt. I sat for a minute, staring straight ahead with my hands on the wheel. Then I turned to Sandy and reached up to remove her sunglasses so I could see her reaction properly. Her eyes were half-closed, heavy-lidded. Closing and opening like the inner lids of some fish.

"What's happened?" she asked.

"Let me check."

I got out and went around to the back of the car. There were little bits of automobile strewn behind us, like a garage sale in the middle of the road. I could see the muffler and bumper and bolts and bits of metal. Also I could see a brake disc and what looked to be part of the rear axle. I had nearly torn off the back of the car, which was an incredible feat.

I walked around to the front and got in the seat next to Cassandra and she opened her eyes to look at me. She was conserving the last of her energy and only talked to me when she had to, and when she did talk she used the minimum number of words to get her point across. She asked what I'd done. I told her flat out that I'd torn the rear axle off the car and that this was a screw-up of catastrophic proportions and that I was so very sorry, and I nearly started crying in my desire to apologize and explain about the rocks and then Sandy said something, cutting me off, and I had to stop to hear as she said it again, after a breath: "Carry me."

*

It was half a mile to Chora and the shore. I did not know if I could carry Sandy that far but of course I had to try. We had to leave everything else: the chains, the weights, the anchor. The only thing I took was the bottle of water, a cloth, and a few strawberries. The morphine drip was nearly done. I gave the bulb one last squeeze and removed the needle from her cannula.

I got out and walked around to my sister's side of the car and swung it open. This time when I hefted her I did so with a real sense of her weight – attempting to gauge how long I could sustain it for. She curled towards me and got an arm around my shoulder and hung it there, her palm pressed to my neck. The white silk of the shroud trailed from her frame and I carried her like that, like a bride, as I walked down the mountain towards the sea.

At first I hummed to myself and to her, as if to prove I could handle it and that I had strength to spare and also to lighten the mood, to dispel the feeling that I had done something terrible and irreparable that would haunt me forever. If I didn't get Cassandra to the sea, I felt she truly would die. The sea was her salvation. The sea was where she belonged.

My sandals flapped on the stony path and the sun slapped hard on the back of my neck and the dust, which seemed to hover over that road like an aura, got in my nostrils and throat, parching me and drying me out. Soon enough I stopped humming and instead simply focused on my breathing, keeping it even and steady as you would if you were running a long race. In and out. In and out. Every three steps. We walked with the hillside on our left – all yellow and tawny stone, yucca plants and scrub – and lemon orchards on the right. Neither gave any protection from the sun, which was getting higher in the sky now and blazing. The air up in the hills was hot and still and stifling, almost tangible. Even the breeze in my face felt hot, like the blast of a fan heater.

There were other sensations, most of them painful. The sting of blisters between my big and index toe, where the thong of my right sandal was rubbing. The burning ache in my biceps at the weight of Sandy, growing heavier at each step. And the wobble-kneed jerking of my legs beneath me, functioning like those of an automaton. Just going and going.

But none of that mattered. I had focus, purpose. I would get her there because I had to get her there. At one point I even started chanting that: I'll get you there, I'll get you there, I'll get you there. Like the Little Engine that Could, telling himself I think I can I think I can I think I can. And I reached a place of equanimity and resolve – past the wall, that marathon runners talk of – where I became certain that I would achieve this, feeling my legs revitalize, my arms revive, my breathing level out.

And that was when I broke my ankle.

*

I broke it pathetically, feebly, in a little hole that some rodent had dug into the road. My sandaled foot went into that and turned neatly sideways and the pain was instant and intense and excruciating, as if the foot had been crushed by a piledriver: this explosive blast of pain.

I gasped and fell and managed not to drop my sister but took the impact on my elbows and rolled sideways onto my shoulder. I had to lay Cassandra down in the road, in the dirt, as I rolled and writhed and fanned at my ankle, miming my animal pain that was too terrible to express. I made silent screams, my mouth wide. The ankle was already fat, swelling, going balloon-like. Tendons torn, bones snapped. The pain did not actually fade but eventually I became inured to it, going into shock, and that allowed me to function more normally.

Sandy, whose glasses had been knocked off her face in the fall, was watching my theatrics with bemusement and sympathy. I had the ignominious task of crawling over to her, to where my sister lay in the dirt, and telling her that I had a bit of an issue, another one, but that I'd think of something – make a splint, maybe, or a crutch out of a stick – though how I'd walk with the crutch and carry her at the same time was something that would need some careful and serious consideration. Then I had the idea (and I was saying all this to her, babbling and slobbering a little, partly delirious) that I could carry her and waddle on my knees the rest of the way. We had to be close. We had to have made it maybe three quarters of the way, or at least halfway – halfway at the very least. Then I had another idea.

"Can you roll?" I asked her.

"Can I roll?"

"You know – roll. Like we used to roll down hills, as a kid."

"I don't think I have it in me to roll."

I lay there panting, my face smeared with sweat and snot and dust, as I considered all the other possibilities, of which there were none.

"I don't think we're going to make it," she said.

"I'm so sorry."

"I think you should just hold me, now."

And so I did. I lay on my back and got my arm under her and cradled her. I was blubbering. Not just from the pain, or the knowledge that she was dying, but also from the realization that I had ruined her last moments in the way I had most feared and also in the way Sandy had probably expected: which was perhaps why she seemed to be taking it all in stride. With me in charge failure and calamity was a distinct possibility. She knew that better than me and was also better at accepting it than me. She'd known it ever since I'd lit the entire house on fire during her sixth birthday party and she'd had to organize the emergency evacuation.

In the sky, I saw a small plane puttering. It was dragging a banner behind it.

"Look," I said.

The banner read, "*Cassandra je t'aime. Mon couer est à toi pour toujours.*"

"Henri," she said.

"You should have brought him instead," I said.

"No," she said, and spat a strand of blood. "It had to be you."

The plane dragged its banner right across the sky and behind the hills, the drone lingering for a time before it, too, faded. I wondered if I would ever see Henri again and what we would say, how we would act, if we did. As I lay wondering that I could feel the flutter of Sandy's breath against me, and the off-kilter thudding of my heart, and the tight, menacing pain in my ankle, which had begun to throb and send stinging pulses up my shin to my knee, as if a jellyfish had latched on down there and was working its tentacles further up my calf. That whole leg felt hot and strange and wrong.

And as we lay there in the dust I began to feel something else. At first I thought it was Sandy's heart, beating against my own. But it grew stronger and then I could almost hear it. I could hear it. It was not in us but outside. A faint tock-tocking like drumsticks tapping, like water dripping, like time resonating. I raised my head and peered down the path, or rather up the path – since I was lying with my head downhill – and between my feet, one straight and one twisted, bent, I saw the man in his cart and his plodding donkey and the faint cloud of yellow dust they brought with them, coming towards us.

*

Later I would think about how odd it must have been for the man, to see the various parts of the car on the road and then the car itself, not just without a bumper or muffler but without an axle, sitting there in the middle of the road, which must have been somewhat difficult for him to manoeuvre around. And then to come further along and find us both lying there, cuddled up, Sandy wrapped in her silk shroud and me red-eyed, whimpering, broken.

Considering all that, he did not seem at all bewildered or even surprised. He walked his donkey passed us – and for a terrible moment I thought he might just keep going, and I cried out feebly – but then the cart stopped. He got down. He was quite spry for an old man and landed easily in the dust. He did not move gingerly or stiffly at all. He crouched next to us and looked at Cassandra, seeming to sense instinctively that she was the one in charge and also that whatever had gone wrong was no doubt my fault. He spoke to her softly in Greek and she said something back. *Thálassa.* The sea, the sea.

Yes, he said, he would take us to the sea.

He had left his shells and stones wherever it was he left them, and was perhaps returning for another load because his cart was empty except for a few blankets and a jug of water. I watched from the ground as he spread the blankets over the bed of the cart and came back to us.

He moved Sandy first, murmuring something to her just before he hefted her and then turning and laying her down on the edge of the cart. Then he got up into the cart himself to position her properly, with her head near his seat.

I was too big for him to lift. He stooped and got one of my arms around his shoulder and with him supporting me like that I managed to stand on my good leg. I hopped over to his cart and he sort of pushed at my buttocks as I squirmed up into the back, wriggling on my belly like an iguana, damaged but still flailing and trying. I got in eventually. As he hopped back into his seat I wormed closer to Sandy. The man was above us now, in the saddle, and looking down. He motioned to Sandy and made a cradling gesture with his arms, as if holding an invisible infant. I understood and eased myself into a sitting position with my back against the side of the cart. Then I moved her head so it was cushioned in my lap. Seeing we were ready, the man took the reins and clicked his tongue and the donkey began to walk. I looked down at my sister. Her eyes were wide and open and they seemed ominously vacant, gazing up at the sky, into the brightness of the sun, and I had that familiar stomach-drop sensation until she asked me if I had any strawberries. I checked my pockets.

"I crushed them all when I fell," I said, miserably.

"What about water?"

I'd left it in the road. But the old man had some. I opened his bottle and splashed a little in my palm, and let it trickle into her mouth. She said that it tasted salty, and I told her that was probably from my sweat, or maybe my tears.

*

On the outskirts of Chora we passed a woman in a hut who sold fresh oranges and jugs of wine. She raised her hand to the driver and shouted out in Greek, possibly asking him where we were going.

"*Thálassa*," our driver called.

That became the chant, the mantra, as we came into town. People asked him and he repeated the phrase. At first he called it out in answer and then he seemed to just be calling it. Thálassa, thálassa, she's going to the sea. Or sometimes their name for her: *erǫméni tis thálassas*. I echoed him. I had Sandy's head cradled in my lap and her hand in mine and though her eyes were closed I knew she was alive because I could see the rise and fall of her breath and the slight smile on her face and I could feel, too, the soft pressure of her hand.

"I can smell the brine," she said, her eyes fluttering open.

It was market day, which I hadn't expected. The stalls were set up and the vendors languished in the shade, with their wares of fishing gear, olive jars, wine, grapes, cheese, bread, scarves, camisoles. We came into the centre of that with our driver pronouncing his decree – *thálassa, thálassa* – and the townsfolk in the market seemed drawn to it. They began trailing along in our wake: first a couple of children, who'd been playing football, and then the fishmonger with the eyepatch, and the old lady who sold embroidery. And others, too. It was if they had been waiting for this, as if they too had known today would be the day.

Many of them had sheets of paper. They held them in both hands, tight across their bellies, and I saw that the sheets were in fact flyers, with Cassandra's photo on the front – looking young and strong and vigorous, standing on some beach and pointing at the horizon.

"Henri's done a flyover," I said. "They all have leaflets about you."

"Nobody here knows English."

"I think they're in French."

"They don't know French, either."

"Maybe they think they're invitations."

She smiled. "To my sending off."

Just being near the sea had made her stronger. She managed to raise her hand, to acknowledge the crowd, in a final grand gesture. They cheered. There were about twenty or thirty people, now, but they all kept a respectful distance, starting a few paces back and then spreading outwards, like a wave rippling away from us. The market was near the marina and our driver drove the cart right out onto the dock – a rickety, creaky old structure jutting into the Aegean. I pointed out our *gaïta*, though he would have known it already: we had taken it out most days, back when Sandy was well enough. He reined in the donkey, halting beside it.

By that point I was lightheaded from the heat and trauma of my ankle, and only partly lucid. I began to crawl to the edge of the cart and then I felt hands on me, touching me and uplifting me, carrying me. Hands beneath me and on my shoulders, and me in the air, my face turned towards the sun-glare, the sky, the heat. And Sandy was coming just behind me. Both of us upheld as if in offering, the whole town lifting us from the cart, passing us one to the other, until we were lowered into the boat: me at the bow and Sandy at the stern.

When our driver made as if to get in too, I held up a hand to him. Thank you, I said, but it's okay. I can do it. He looked at me then, and smiled – showing those white teeth of his – and tipped his flatcap. He removed his foot from the bottom of the boat and untied the bowline. I got myself into position and fitted the oarlocks. Sandy curled up, serenely, in the stern. She was gazing at the bay, dappled with waves that flicker-flared in the midday sun.

"Let me touch the water," she said.

I put her hand over the side, so that her fingers were trailing below the surface. Then I held my palm up to the driver, the kids, and the rest of the townsfolk. I began to row and the motion didn't aggravate my ankle. As we drew away from the dock the crowd began to sing. The words were lost to me, but the music floating over the water sounded ancient and timeless as the sea itself, as the blood beating in my ears. The choral ode of Chora.

"We made it, Puck," Cassandra said.

I was crying, of course. But not only from grief.

"We don't have the chains or anchor or anything," I said.

"It doesn't matter," she said. "Just put me in the water, when the time comes."

"Sandy," I said, nearly whimpering. "Cassandra."

I let the oars go limp, and tried to move closer to her. It wasn't easy, in a narrow boat, with my bad ankle. I rose up and lurched and fell towards her, the hull wobbling beneath me, and as I caught hold of her we went over – splash – dumped into a shock of water, warm as a bathtub, warm as a womb. I clung to her, horrified that I'd ruined her final perfect moment, until I saw the bubbles escaping from her mouth, and heard her laughing at me underwater.

Nikesh Shukla

Author of A Man, Without a Donkey

Nikesh Shukla is the author of the critically acclaimed novel Meatspace, the Costa-shortlisted novel Coconut Unlimited and the award-winning novella The Time Machine. He wrote the short film Two Dosas and the Channel 4 sitcom Kabadasses.

Twitter: @nikeshshukla

A Man,
Without a
Donkey

La-la salama, Raks sings to himself. It's the only line of the song he knows and it's been rattling around his head since the boy sailing the dhow sang it as he tipped Naman's ashes into the Indian Ocean. He asked what it meant. *Sleep well, now,* the boy replied, and Raks smiled. Not because it was a poignant moment, but because he didn't know how else to act.

He wrote the words down in the back of his guidebook. When he was done with the urn, he left it on the floor of the dhow. The boy asked if he could have it. Raks nodded. As the dhow cut through the water, the sun glinting off the waves like television static, giving it the shimmer of bad reception, the boy plunged the urn into the ocean and swilled out the last particles of Naman. Once he was satisfied, he placed the urn and its lid under the bench Raks sat on. *Good for carrying water,* the boy said. He smiled. *Pole-pole* he said to Raks. It meant *slowly-slowly.*

Raks hasn't spoken to his father in a week. He'll be worried. Raks is in Lamu, which wasn't the plan. He wanted to visit the donkey sanctuary and deliver the cheque from Naman's estate in person, rather than send a cheque. For all the Little Vijays out there, Naman specified in the will. Little Vijay was a donkey, Raks' dad had adopted for him as a child. Naman had fallen in love with it on a family trip to Devon. Up for adoption, Little Vijay was described as 'anarchic'. Maybe no one has adopted it, Naman said, because it has an Indian name. I want to adopt it.

Raks is bewildered by Lamu. It's an island operated by donkeys. There is no transportation. It's either foot or saddle. He's sitting with a beer, watching people get on and off the island in the harbour and he's worrying about money. He left a suitcase of things at the hotel he's staying at in Mombasa, things he wouldn't need on a weekend trip to Lamu. He left his passport. He can't withdraw any money without his passport. Kenyan bureaucracy likes that element of authority. There are no ATMs. He has to go into the branch, show two pieces of ID to the bank manager, along with his bankcard, and sign three pieces of paper. He doesn't have the requisite amount of ID. He has been refused money.

He is here for twelve more hours. He has enough shillings for three more beers. He hasn't eaten all day. A bowl of rice and cabbage he ate on the road at one of the stops has been churning in his stomach since he arrived yesterday. He hopes a beer will settle it. This one might have to last him all night. He watches as donkeys waddle past, laden with tourists or saddlebags of concrete. He watches as sailors try and convince the white tourists to ride out on their boats for fishing or swimming or romance. Or all three. The Triple Threat Boat Trip. He stares at his watch and wills the next twelve hours to be over.

"Another beer, sir?" the waiter asks.

He shakes his head. "I'm fine."

"Very good, sir," the waiter replies. "Stay as long as you need."

"Thanks."

He checks his phone again. Thankfully, he has found a place with free Wi-Fi. He has access to his social networks and to the football results. Solitude never means being alone anymore. It just means being by yourself.

When dad joins him in a few days, he'll be fleetingly annoyed that Raks scattered the ashes without him but that'll soon disappear in the excitement about showing him where he grew up and all the dysfunction of their family dynamic will have travelled the globe.

Dad said to him, "You're going to Kenya? I have to come with you. I have to see the place one last time."

"I'm happy to go by myself," Raks replied.

"Don't you want to see where your father grew up?"

"I'm just going to honour Naman's last wishes, dad. I'm not there for a jolly."

"Why not make it jolly? I will come with you."

"You sure?"

"I am very sure. I want to go home," dad said. "I never thought I could."

Raks spots a girl at the bar. She's white, and a traveller - this much Raks can tell by the beaded anklet she's wearing, and the scarf tying her hair up into a bun. Also, those sunglasses, they look like Ray-Bans. She's betraying the traveller look with this nod to hipsterism. A Jackson Pollock of freckles covers her neck and cheeks. Her white linen shirt, dirtied by the dust of Lamu, is open down to her chest and dotted with more freckled sun-blushes. She sips on a fruit juice. Raks notices she smokes. After ten minutes of tracing the freckles in his mind, he takes a cigarette out of the packet on the table and walks over and asks for a light. She smiles and silently fishes one out of a bottomless hessian bag she has tied around her front like it's a sleeping baby swathed in ethnic cloth. Raks lights his cigarette and hands her back her lighter. "Thanks," he says, hoping she's American or Canadian, he loves those accents.

"Pleasure," she says in a miscellaneous European accent.

"French?" Raks asks.

"German," she replies, pulling out a book from her bottomless bag as if to indicate this is what she would rather be doing.

"I'm English," Raks says. "But don't hold that against me."

"You don't look English," she replies.

"I'm Raks."

'You sound Indian."

"I am. What's your name?"

"Ingrid," she says, sighing, looking around for help. She angles her body and head away from Raks, having to turn around uncomfortably to answer any of his questions.

"Like the Bride of Dracula," Raks says.

Ingrid turns around to face him. "Yes, as a matter of fact. I'm named after Ingrid Pitman. My father was a fan of Hammer Horror films." She laughs. "People always say Bergman. Not Pitt. I'm impressed. What did you say your name was?"

"Raks," he says. "I'm not named after anyone famous." He shakes her hand. It's dry and small. "Maybe a Bollywood star you've never heard of…"

"Rakesh Roshan, maybe?" Ingrid says. Raks laughs.

"Touché," he says. She smiles at him and gestures for him to join her.

"What brought you to Lamu?" she asks.

"It's the opposite of technology," he says. "I thought I could disconnect from the world."

"They have free Wi-Fi at this bar."

"Yes," Raks says. "Thank god."

"What do you think of the donkeys?" Ingrid asks. Raks thinks for a moment. He feels like he needs to have a big symbolic opinion about them, but he sees them as functional.

"A man without a donkey is a donkey," he says, repeating the line from the wall of the donkey sanctuary he visited earlier.

She nods. "I know," she replies. "Those of us who face our burdens alone, we're doomed to a life of misery."

"Exactly," Raks says, glad she has given him the context for a big opinion, one he saw on a wall. Next to the quote, in smaller letters, it said 'Swahili proverb'. Raks had written the quote in the back of his guidebook, underneath *La-la salama*, thinking this will be a weird proverb to throw at people in strange situations in the future.

Raks brought the cheque to the donkey sanctuary this afternoon, causing chaos by arriving with unsolicited money. A faceless figure, stood on the balcony, threw the cap of a beer bottle at him as he opened the gate of the small sanctuary and entered the courtyard teeming with donkeys. It hit his head. Another faceless figure laughed like it was the funniest thing he had ever seen. Raks said he was in possession of a donation, to a woman wearing a lab coat, tending to a donkey and she had smiled at him as she pulled out a mobile phone and sent a text she wrote without breaking her smile or her eye contact with him. Moments later, someone called Mrs Bridge arrived and made him sign the cheque directly over to her. She showed him around the donkey stables and he explained to her the achievements of the donkey sanctuary's newest benefactor. He made Naman sound like the model cousin, an eccentric computer genius with a heart of gold, rather than the difficult acerbic nerd Raks saw at family functions. Mrs Bridge smiled like she cared about the man behind the money. When Raks gave her the cheque she smelt it and put it in her pocket without looking at it.

"Little Vijay is here," Mrs Bridge said. "Would you like to see him?"

"I'd love to."

She showed him the enclosure for Little Vijay. Little Vijay had a name tag that said Mala. Mala was female.

Mrs Bridge showed Raks into the enclosure and he had half-heartedly petted Mala, keeping up the pretence. She had a dribbling nose. One eyelid was half-closed. She was panting. She wasn't Little Vijay. Raks blew on her nose like he was told to. To show he was friendly. He had approached her from the side as instructed. As he blew, she shuddered and walked forward till his eye and nose line were squat with her bottom. Mrs Bridge shrugged.

"She is having a difficult day."

Now Raks is running out of money, he wishes he hadn't given 'Little Vijay' three thousand guilty Kenyan shillings because Mrs Bridge had said that Little Vijay had a degenerative disease and she couldn't afford the injection to make him/Mala feel better. He had spent two thousand more shillings on a t-shirt and a water bottle.

"I can't get any money out," he says. "I went to the cash machine and they wouldn't give me any cash. There's only one cash machine on the island..."

"Everything is through cash," she says, smiling as if she's been stung by this before. "What are you going to do? Unless this is you asking me for money. Which would be uncool. Slick. But uncool."

"I leave in twelve hours. I have to entertain myself till then."

"I am your entertainment."

"Is that a question or a request?" She smiles. "Seriously," he says. "Don't feel like you have to talk to me or hang out with me. I'm just passing the time with a beautiful woman. Terrible way to spend an evening." That's what he calls the compli-cation. He sandwiches a compliment in amongst two self-deprecating insults about himself. It works because she reaches forward and touches his hand to show him she's not that bothered by his company.

Ingrid puts her book back in her bag and stands up. "I want to show you something."

"Anything." Raks feels the Wi-Fi kick in his pocket, with the vibration of another notification.

Raks wore a bowtie to Naman's funeral because he wanted to stand out. Not that he'd admit it, he wanted his cousins to look at him and think, 'Wow, that Raks is one stylish dude'.

Raks had the eulogy in his pocket. He was going to read Puff Daddy's verse from I'll Be Missing You and say some things about Naman's genius. Standing in front of his family, being the conspicuous one in a bowtie, being the one who had organized everything, he didn't account for the flurry of emotion that came with realising everyone was looking at him and the room was silent for the first time in days. He read the first line on the page, 'Everyday I wake up I hope I'm dreaming,' and sat down, crying. His cousin Rekha had to read his speech out and she missed all the inflections, emphases and jokes, speaking in a flat monotone, dreary voice. Naman was committed to the fire and they went back to Raks' dad's house for bowls of pho, Naman's favourite food, and a nice New Zealand pink, zesty and summery with a hint of Grenache.

Raks sat in the corner in a foul mood, upset he hadn't been able to deliver the memorable eulogy he'd planned. The rest of the family had a lovely time despite his sour face. They didn't know Naman. They didn't get him. The fact that he was dead meant little to them. They were there to catch up with each other. It was not like someone pivotal to the family has died, they secretly thought. This wasn't an emotion vocally expressed. It was a general feeling – he didn't have much to do with us. We're here out of obligation and to see each other.

The day after the funeral, Raks woke up with a hangover. He'd spent the night at Naman's, going through his things and drinking his way through old bottles of Naman's wine club delivery, ones he had found next to Naman's bed, which stank of cigarettes. He managed half a bottle of white on an empty stomach before he was blotto and had to lie down on the sofa. The particulars of Naman's will dictated that everything be given to charity unless Raks wanted anything. Raks took the books, mostly programming textbooks he didn't understand, to the charity shop. He took Naman's clothes to a clothes bank and he was left with an impressive amount of alcohol, an empty fridge, DVD boxsets and computer equipment.

In the flat by himself, he looked around at all the things Naman surrounded himself with so he didn't feel lonely. The toys, the boxsets, the wine. Everything in the flat pointed to the computer and the plasma screen mounted on the wall above it. When Naman wanted to watch things, he'd load them up on the computer, turn the plasma on and lie back on that uncomfortable sofa that only seated two people. Raks thought about his own place, and the independence he had. He felt lonely a lot, so he went to the pub most nights. He never cooked in the kitchen. He had his two acoustic guitars and that unread series of Game of Thrones books and his Sky account. It was almost like he was Naman. At least Naman was happy. Raks spent a lot of time wishing he could move back home. He'd made such a fuss of moving out, there was no way he would attempt that backtrack.

Ingrid leads Raks away from the bar. He steals a quick look at his phone, at the bars of Wi-Fi slipping away, and then ten steps away, he goes dark. No signal. He has to exist in the moment.

People wear white on this island. It's hot.

The white reflects the sunlight but it also makes things a lot brighter for a guy who has forgotten his sunglasses. He squints as Ingrid leads him along the water front, the high street that runs the length of the island. He walks past donkeys and tourists and beach boys. The water glistens. The top of Ingrid's back is freckled and pink. Raks likes how he only notices things when his phone is off. He follows her, a step behind and admires how she sidesteps people trying to sell her things. She has a firm hand to say no thanks. She turns to him.

"I got to the island two weeks ago and I've just shut down. I'm on automatic pilot now."

"Are you travelling?"

"I'm seeing the world before…" she stops. "I just realised I haven't really spoken to anyone in two weeks. I was about to tell you all my secrets."

"I can keep a secret."

"It's not whether you can keep it… it's whether you should know it in the first place."

"I'll tell you one of my own.'

"It's nice not having to work isn't it? I haven't had to work in three weeks now. Not since I left for Kenya. I mean, the beauty of this country is majestic isn't it? Everything in its right place at its own speed with its own wings of flight," she says. *Pole-pole.*

"You're talking about us, right? As tourists?"

Ingrid stops and looks at him. "We're not tourists," she says. Oh no, Raks thinks, I've befriended a hippy. "Look at everyone," she says. "They look so happy."

"Just because we're out here in this traveller bubble and we see everyone smiling because they want us to buy something from them, doesn't mean they're not all struggling, working hard behind the scenes, living in poverty, hoping that dumb Westerners like us will come and spend money on their tat, just so they can live." Raks says.

"You're very cynical. And this is as much a stereotype as my one. My one is a nicer one to sit behind." Ingrid turns away from Raks, as if she's considering the onward journey and whether she even wants to do it anymore. She looks at Raks. He has dark circles under his eyes and he hasn't shaved in a week. He looks sad and bloated, she thinks. She wants to strip all of that away in the same way it was stripped away for her. "Come on, then," she says.

"Where are you taking me?" he asks.

"That is definitely a secret." She pauses. "Are you with anyone?"

"How do you mean? A girlfriend? No. Not me. No time. You?"

"I don't have a girlfriend, no," she says and laughs. "Or a boyfriend. Or anyone. No one in the world knows where I am right now. What about you?"

"No. Nor me. I'm supposed to be in Mombasa. My hotel has Wi-Fi.

I'm supposed to check in with my dad."

"What brought you here?"

"The donkeys," Raks says.

Ingrid turns off the main street on to a side one. The houses here are close together. It feels European with its higgledy-piggledy white and beige building fronts. The people on the streets away from the sea front are distinctly darker than Raks has noticed in the town. These are the real people, he thinks. Kenyans.

A shudder of panic creeps over him and he wonders whether he should have exercised caution when going off with a strange woman, maybe paid a little attention to the direction she has led him in. She seems benevolent and kind. He doesn't need to be paranoid. His dad filled him with paranoid advice before he left, like keeping his money in his shoe and his pants. Don't wear a watch or the thick silver chain he has been known to be partial to. His dad was horrified when he found out Raks wore boxers, which meant it would be impossible to keep money in there. He was instructed not to carry his wallet and not take his phone out. The last one annoyed him the most.

"Everyone has phones now. Why would anyone want my one? It's two models old."

"Just listen to me, these are my people," Raks father said angrily. He had been angry non-stop ever since it happened, taking any opportunity to not show any weakness.

"You haven't lived in Kenya for over forty years," Raks replied. "Places change."

"People do not."

"Yes, you haven't changed. Your opinions are from the 60s."

Ingrid asks what Raks is doing in Kenya. He tells her about Naman, about his ashes.

"I'm so sorry about your cousin."

"Thanks, he was annoying when he was alive. Really annoying. But we grew up together. And I miss him so much. You forget to always appreciate what a constant people are for you."

"I don't know what it is to lose someone so close to you. I've been lucky."

"What about you? What brings you here?"

"Death," she says. She pauses. "I was told this story down in the docks yesterday. I can't get it out of my head. In the beginning there was no death. This is the story of how death came into the world. There was once a man known as Leeyio who was the first man that Naiteru-kop brought to earth. Naiteru-Kop then called Leeyio and said to him: 'When a man dies and you dispose of the corpse, you must remember to say, man die and come back again, moon die, and remain away.' Many months elapsed before anyone died. When, in the end, a neighbour's child did die, Leeyio was summoned to dispose of the body. When he took the corpse outside, he made a mistake and said: 'Moon die and come back again, man die and stay away.' So after that no man survived death. A few more months elapsed, and Leeyio's own child went missing. So the father took the corpse outside and said: 'Moon die and remain away, man die and come back again.' On hearing this, Naiteru-kop said to Leeyio: 'You are too late now for, through your own mistake, death was born the day when your neighbour's child died.' So that is how death came about, and that is why up to this day when a man dies he does not return, but when the moon dies, it always comes back again."

Raks smiles. "My dad used to tell me something similar but he'd put his finger to his lips and say, tell no-one. We're Hindu, not Kikuyu."

"The Masaai don't say a person is dead. They say they are asleep. I like that. The idea of a big snooze."

"My cousin never slept. He'd stay awake all night drinking and watching Star Trek. He was a soldier to booze."

"Is that what killed him?"

"No, he had cancer, which we didn't even know about until he died. A big cancerous growth in his left lung. Funny thing is, that's not what killed him either. He fell getting off a bus and wouldn't stop bleeding."

Ingrid smiles. "I like the romance of that. He didn't fall in the lake or the ocean. He died at a bus stop."

"It's not romantic."

She leads Raks past a sandpit and through an archway. They are on sand now. On the sand, flecks of dried seaweed and palm tree flap in the wind. Ingrid takes her shoes off and holds them. Raks stares at her feet. He has a compulsion to stare at feet whenever they're bare. Not because he has a foot fetish but to check they are friendly normal toes. They were painted red months ago. They're chipped with usage.

Ingrid notices him staring and as they clomp through the sand.

"You're a foot fetishist," Ingrid says, laughing.

He shakes his head. "I'm not. Every since I was a kid, I check people's feet to see how friendly they are. You can tell a lot about someone from their toes. It's just a weird thing I do. I don't want to fuck anyone's feet."

The swear word hangs in the air as they reach the top of the dune. The beach is immaculate. It's empty, the sea is purple in the overcast mugginess, untrodden sand.

"What do mine tell you?"

"You're worn out," Raks says.

Ingrid laughs. "You're so right."

Ingrid runs down the incline of the dune and Raks, removing his shoes, follows, plunging his own feet deep into the sand.

He runs down the incline, his hands aloft, his backpack bouncing up and down his back. If he had troubles, they are blasted in the face by the warm sea breeze that greets his momentum. Hot sand scatters like buckshot across his calves, his toes melting into the cool clusters underneath. Ingrid is tearing off her clothes as she runs. She's wearing a bikini underneath her long-sleeved t-shirt and linen trousers. She pulls off the bandana and a golden explosion of red hair explodes over her shoulders. She has a tattoo of a tree across her back. It's spindly, black and ominous but in its silhouette flutter the fragrances of deep red blossom. She dives into the water, is underneath for ten long seconds and comes out fifty metres into the sea. She beckons to him. Raks stops running at the water's edge. Its shallows caress his toes. The water is warm.

"Come on in," Ingrid shouting, beckoning with splashes of water.

It doesn't take much for Raks to take his t-shirt and shorts off. He's wearing the same boxers he arrived with. They're tight and they're white, a big mistake for the occasional upset stomach this trip has given him. They could do with a swill. Raks puts his shorts and things on top of his bag and runs in. He keeps turning his head back to his things hoping they won't be taken. There's not a lot he can do if they are.

He dives into the water. It's warm and cooling at the same time. He feels like he's swimming in bubbly bath water. He isn't a strong swimmer. His kick was his problem. With his strong arms he wades his way to Ingrid. They look back at the coast.

"No one ever comes here," she says.

"Why not? It's beautiful." Raks can see the ruins of a castle to his left, the fringes of the town to his right.

"There was a shark sighting a few years ago. Now it's deserted."

"The Indian Ocean's too warm for sharks, right?"

"That's why I come here."

Raks wades closer to Ingrid, their fingers and limbs close enough to touch as they tread water in sync. He turns to face her. She continues to look at the beach.

"Don't."

"Don't what?"

"Please," Ingrid says. "That isn't what this is." She pulls off the wig. She's bald. There are wisps of red hair where it's tried to grow back but the hair is gone and her scalp is white, there is a thick tan line between her face and hairline. It's bumpy and you can almost see the blood pumping underneath its alabaster cling film around her crown. She smiles at Raks. Raks feels his stomach lurch and he hesitates, submerging slightly and swallowing water in surprise.

"How far along are you?"

"I have days left. Well, I had months left months ago so it must be days now."

"Why aren't you at home?"

"It's complicated."

"Everything's complicated. It's simple too," Raks says.

"Okay, well, it's none of your business."

"What are you doing?"

"Out here? I'm living in paradise. With the donkeys and the beautiful people, eating fresh mangoes and avocadoes, relaxing, whatever I choose. I am a donkey."

"But you're by yourself."

"On all roads we are alone," Ingrid says and lies back so her ears are submerged in the bobbing water and she is floating.

Raks sees two boys approach his things. He starts wading back towards the shore till he can stand. One of them kicks at his shorts and t-shirt and the other one slides out the bag. Raks starts running forward and they peel off, one with his clothes, the other with his bag. He goes for his bag. As he runs out of the water, his white boxers cling to him, translucent and heavy. He runs after the boy who is running in swerves, back and forth, to confuse him. Raks is wise to his game, fast and in a straight line so manages to launch himself on the boy as he bobs up across the dune. They both clatter into the sand. It's hot and it burns their skin, Raks' more so because he is slick with damp water. The boy yells and Raks puts all his weight on him as he takes the bag off him. The boy stares at Raks, scared.

Raks takes his bag and puts it on his back, the gristle of sand rubbing at his skin.

"Sorry, mister," the boy says.

"It's fine, little man," Raks says.

The boy holds his hand out for money. Raks smiles. The boy smiles and gets up, still holding his hand out. Raks lets out a laugh and turns round to face where he's come from. He hears the boy scamper off. He can see his clothes not far from where he left them, discarded, taken as misdirection. He goes to retrieve them and tell Ingrid he's going. He walks back to the spot where he left his things. He can see her flip-flops bobbing on the wades of the water so moves them back. He walks over to his t-shirt and shorts and picks them up, returning them back to where they should be. He looks out to see where Ingrid is. He can't see her anywhere. He shouts out her name but she doesn't reply.

The water is clear. There are no boats, no swimmers, no signs of life. She has disappeared from view. He wonders whether to wait for her. He wants to swim out and look for her but there's no point. The beach and the water are flat. There is no incline and he can see a fair way into the distance. She isn't there. She's gone.

The water jingles in limp perpetual motion. He stands at the edge of the sand looking out into the world. She's gone. In the distance, he can hear a donkey bray.

He looks down at his feet, the imprinted contours they've made in the sand. Bobbing next to them is a lump of hair. It makes him jump and he moves away from it, thinking it an animal. It's Ingrid's wig. It's lifeless now and though it may have been sun-streaked by excessive blasts of light in this paradise, now it is a wig without a place to call home.

At a loss for anything to do, Raks takes his phone out of his pocket and texts his father that he can't wait to see him. As he types out the letters, he sings to himself. *La-la salama.* Sleep well soon.

Frances Gapper

Author of The Moustache Maker's Daughter

Frances Gapper's two story collections are The Tiny Key (Sylph Editions, 2009) and Absent Kisses (Diva Books, 2002). Other stories have found homes in two issues of Short Fiction journal, the London Magazine online, the Reader's Digest and The Moth. Her third collection, In the Wild Wood, will be published in 2017 by Cultured Llama.

The Moustache Maker's Daughter

Lucy is my name, which means light, and my dad is Ludicrous the moustache maker, so I am Lucy Ludicrous. As a girl, I moulded light into many a useful or pleasing form, dazzling the unwary by making sunbeams zip round corners and scattering sparkles from my fingertips to glitter enticingly on my skin and clothes. Since then I have grown wiser, though I still love a joke. I now intend in all seriousness to describe my life, or at least one day of it – setting the honest truth down here in my occasional book.

The dew is lit by an egg yolk sun just lifted over next-door's chimney, a sun getting ready to fry itself for breakfast with bacon, mushrooms, tomatoes and black pudding, all served on a sky-blue plate. Or anyway, such is my fancy. In a spirit of devilish nonsense, later to be regretted, I conjure up some thistledown baubles and skim them over our neighbour's fence to frizzle his begonias.

I'm on my way to Dad's workshop. As usual I glance up at the house roof, remembering how Mam slipped off it while gathering moss for our Organic Adventures range of moustaches, constructed from natural non-hair materials. Whether her curses (shrieked during her fatal fall) brought bad luck or the century-end just wasn't the right time to launch such an innovative concept, sadly either way the new line failed to interest our customers. Mam is buried in the churchyard, a stylised moustache carved over her dates and name, Tootsie Ludicrous. The broken gutter she clutched at desperately still hasn't been mended and in consequence there's now a damp patch on my bedroom ceiling. This is what it's like living with Dad, a man so obsessed by his craft and with profit and loss, he takes no practical steps to weatherproof our dwelling-place.

Having wiped my boots on the tired mat, worn thin from the pressure of many feet (feet that toil here from sunup to sundown and feet of a superior stamp that come to view the moustaches or attend fittings), my first task is to sweep the workshop. Tiny fragments of hair arise from the broom in a prickly cloud and make me sneeze violently while emptying my dustpan into the incinerator.

Next I check that none of the moustaches have been stolen or eaten by rats. Pinned to boards in glass cases like dead insects, they are arranged in six main groups: the Natural, the Hungarian, the Dalí, the English, the Imperial, the Freestyle. Last night after tea Dad plodded off to the workshop and here on the finishing stand is the result of his midnight labours – a fine handlebar, flaunting its bushy exuberance.

Just as I'm blowing on it lightly to add a pleasing lustre, far better than the artificial conditioning imparted by styling mousse or gel, Dad bangs open the door. He grumpily warns me to be careful and not light it up like a gin palace, then falls to working a great pair of 18th century bellows, of crumbly leather and rusty iron. Although unnecessary, since our furnace is connected to the electricity supply, the daily exercise soothes his temper.

Meanwhile and more usefully, for internet orders make up a sizeable part of our business, I fire up the Amstrad; the modem plays its sad violin. A number of today's requests have been discreetly sent in by hair studios, on behalf of third parties – a member of the Indian police force, a couple of high-profile Middle Eastern politicians. I must also keep in regular contact with our suppliers (experienced moustache growers or outsourcers of growth), dealing with logistics issues and any other problems as they arise. Each supplier is represented by a bobble-headed pin on the map behind my computer. Trondheim has a good sprinkling, also Berlin, Ystad, Anchorage, plus smaller centres of industry such as

Thuringia, Zollernalbkreis and Calw. The best coarse moustaches are grown in Siberia, fine-haired ones by Sikh ladies in the West Midlands.

At eleven we take a posset break. Earlier I concocted two healthful possets and these I now pour from a vacuum flask into our moustache-protector mugs, an abandoned sideline. A knock at the door: I startle and Dad spits posset. Enter a gentleman with a high collar and loose fall of necktie, quite the dandy. And come with a view to purchase, for he's young yet, wishful and fretting, only baby down on his upper lip. Yet he has an excellent mouth for a moustache – this I say not snidely but admiring. His face only lacks one hairy ornament to be perfection (I discount beards, which although they complement our craft are repulsive to me personally). Elsewise he's the excelsior.

"What do you want?" Dad barks at our prospective customer.

He speaks out bold: "a moustache."

"Well you've come to the right place," I say with loud cheerfulness, to drown out Dad.

"Thank you. I hope so." His eye lights on the finishing stand and my parent's new creation. Awed, he ventures near and asks permission to touch. Dad shrugs – his most fulsome gesture of civility.

Our Adonis is enraptured by the handlebar and only unwillingly dissuaded from its purchase. His face is unsuited to this item; I tell him bluntly. Its ideal wearer is a carnival strongman or medal-decorated veteran, or failing one of those a grizzled père de famille. He then ponders a Pancho Villa, foolishly fingers a Fu Manchu. But guided by me, he at last opts for a classic Chevron: suave yet possessed of gravitas, exactly the right follicular architecture for a baby face. And as 'twas ever truly said, the moustache maketh the man.

Dad triples the recommended retail price, adds a double service charge (accounting for us both) and VAT (which we're not registered for) plus a large 'courtesy gratuity'. Presenting our card reader, I bashfully avert my gaze while the Chevron inserts his Mastercard and taps in the code. Et voilà! I fold the receipt of our transaction into his palm. We send him off happy, with a clanking carrier bagful of salves and potions.

"Well, Dad" I say jokingly, "your new handlebar is king of our collection."

A smile creeps to one corner of Dad's mouth and nestles there, like a dormouse in winter, as he shakes his head. Undeniably the handlebar is a mo with mojo, but: "I've known better," he says. "Ah. Once I made a moustache to go courting in. Got a hedge wizard to put a glamour on it. Sunlight broke through rain at the moment he cast the spell and it took strong. The moustache leapt to my lip and fixed itself. Down the road I saw a pretty lass and tipped her a wink. Your mam."

His tale makes me guffaw, yet prompts sad reflection on how time destroys our appearances. For that saucy young coxcomb is now a wreck of a man. "What happened to the moustache, Dad?" I ask.

"Duty done, it scarpered. Never laid eyes on it since." Off he goes to the alehouse, to make our profits behave likewise. I sigh, put all in order and lock up, cogitating the while on that tricksy moustache. For sure it pulled the wool over Mam's eyes – a saying that also concerns false hair, as it derives from the ancient practice of tilting an opponent's wig.

But to think of my grumbly old dad playing Prince Charming! A-chortle at this idea, I go in search of the garments he wore in his jaunty youth. I guess they'll still be in his clothes chest, and sure enough. In a twinkling I exchange womanish for mannish apparel. Peering in the mould-spotted glass, I nod at myself. S/he only lacks one vital accessory, I think, but then my nostrils twitch, prompting me to look again. I've gained – and my reflection has too – a moustache! What type of moustache? Hard to say, for it keeps subtly changing, as though to avoid definition. If pressed I'd have to term it the Elusive.

Well! All kitted out and male-beautified, it'd be a shame to hide indoors. So I saunter into the centre, which takes nine minutes. Chainstored much like everywhere else, our town's only novelty feature is its rustic benches. These are fixed with their backs to the road, annoying the old folk, who would rather sit watching the traffic than be knee-bumped by passing shoppers. However, today one of these shunned benches hosts a courting couple: blonde Susie and the Chevron. As I draw closer, Susie spots me too and her pansy eyes open eloquently wide. You wait years for an attractive man to enter the vicinity and then along come two at once! Unlike our local bus service, which is on the whole regular and reliable.

The Chevron struggles under a disadvantage – his moustache is falling off. (Cheap glue's to blame for its slippage: I silently curse my absent parent.) Holding it in place with one finger, he strives to appear at perfect ease. Susie's glance wavers between us, she seems inclined to favour yours truly. I stare hard in the butcher's shop window – pale chitterlings and even paler tripe, faggots in their white webs – then I duck into the baker's.

Behind the display counter is Nush, my old school pal, stout of figure and pretty of face. I pull at my moustache, studying her pastries, pies and patties, her tartlets, quiches and mini-pizzas. Muffins and turnovers, calzone and kugelhopf, Parmesan biscuits and spinachy spanakopita. Chocolate brownies and gingerbread houses, pink eclairs and lemon cupcakes. Her strawberry meringue kisses, her marmalade tray bake.

"Anything take your fancy?"

"I'm still deciding."

"Today's specials..." she begins. Laughter chokes information. Of course she knows me. We sat at the same double desk in the pre-fab classroom and I stuck paper moustaches on my face to amuse her. She cracked up when they fell off.

"A selection?"

"Please."

She pops in an extra cheddar scroll and spins the bag around, twisting its corners. Meanwhile I search the pockets of young-Dad's costume, hoping to light upon a florin or doubloon. But no, empty.

"Um."

"I wouldn't think of charging you. Have a nice day."

I stumble away quite dizzy, whether from the oven's heat or the touch of her fingers. Before exiting, I turn and wink. The moustache twirls as male magic muscles in; Nush gasps and claps a hand under her breast. Too late, the caged bird's flown.

Susie's been watching the door, so as I emerge I'm caught between a rock and a soft place (which of these endures?). But I fail inspection; the blonde huffs in disappointment. I'm sans moustache, is the reason: duty done, it's vanished. Synchronically and right opposite, Dad lurches through the swing doors of the Cock and Anchor. Fearful of him seeing me and consequent tedious explanation, or a medical disaster, I dip and dive, scoot and skedaddle (ancient meaning, to avoid Dad).

Eventide. Restored to womanish dishevelment, I'm sitting in our garden. Nature's fade bestows quiet though un-prayerful reflection. I watch the fat sun crossly squeeze between two 'detached' houses on the new estate. Remembering that long-ago time when Mam and I, perched in the sand dunes, saw it melt gleaming gold into the sea. Mam then arose and shook her skirts. "That's it," she said, ever practical, dismissing melancholy. And the wind blew chill as we stumbled back to our B&B.

I hear a pattering – rain? Small things falling all around, impact of the compact. One strikes my nose, tumbles into my lap. A slug. Neighbour's tossing them over, not in compliment but as revenge missiles. Cautiously I creep to the fence, put my eye to a punched-out knothole. His back door slams. I observe florals all singed and sickly, begonias begone.

Shame on you, Lucy – more rightly to be called Lucifer! That poor man hid his heart among red and white blossoms, therein located the Lovely. And you have pulverised them!

Humbly repentant and mentally scheduling a visit to the garden centre, I pick up the slugs (using my light-generating powers to find where they've fallen) bucket them and set out for the park. I cut down Mudd Lane to Fourways, where a lamppost now stands in place of the old gallows. And leaning against that lamppost is the Chevron.

I bid him good evening, he answers politely, we converse and he soon tells me the reason he's hanging around (ha ha). Since the town has no decent eateries, Susie arranged to meet him later and went home for her tea. We chat jollily, our eyes exchanging romantic suggestions. I perceive that I might have him. Unluckily at this point I make a crude joke about penises, tipping the bucket to reveal its wriggly contents. He turns faint and slides down the lamppost. Ah well.

His moustache is awry. Which reminds me, earlier I purloined a bottle of our best glue from Dad's secret stash. I tuck this into his pocket and leave him to Susie.

Lucy Ludicrous, I sigh, your love of jesting will be your ruination. But then I think of Nush and her cinnamon and raisin swirl cake, whereupon I grin and go on my way, bucket swinging. Tis fine to be merry-alive and running an independent business, in the early 21st century.

Damien Knightley

Author of The Colorado River Toad and the Racoon

Damien Knightley is a London based writer who studied in Leeds, specializing in art, design and book publishing. He has hosted seminars and workshops on the subject of experimental writing techniques and taught writing classes to secondary school students. As well as short fiction he also writes poetry and has been published both in the UK and America. He is currently working on his first screenplay which is now in pre-production. Filming is scheduled to begin in summer 2016.

Website: mrdknightley.wordpress.com

The Colorado River Toad and the Racoon

Part I

Emilia Rose Parker is speaking. The intonation of her voice dances across her tongue and out of her mouth like a blown dandelion. The ruderals manifest hypnotically into the words "You are a Colorado River Toad."

The Colorado River Toad (Incilius alvarius) is a psychoactive toad found in northern Mexico and the southwestern United States. Its skin and venom contain DMT and bufotenin. Both of these chemicals belong to the family of hallucinogenic tryptamines. After inhalation users experience a warm sensation, euphoria, insomnia and strong auditory and visual hallucinations.

Emilia Rose Parker has outdone me again. I cannot think what she would be were she an animal. I should have made sure to have an answer before I posed the question.

At this point me and Emilia Rose Parker are yet to meet in person but I am optimistic that one day very soon we will. Then these wonderful yet frustrating phone calls and ever lasting question and answer sessions will become a gentle footnote in the weighty novel that will be our life together. Something to tell the grandkids. Every time I glimpse reality she says something like "You are a Colorado River Toad" and I find myself on my knees again, howling at the moon. There's a good chance that she'll be the death of me or they'll at least find me naked in a supermarket covered in cat food and singing into a broken whiskey bottle. I kind of hope they do. I've been waiting too long for nothing to happen.

"I will meet you, I promise. I'm going to make it worth your while. It's all I want, all I can think about. I just need to sort some things out. We have forever." This is her mantra, she says it often and I believe her.

Me and Emilia Rose Parker began talking to each other by means of a dating website. She messaged me first to ask me what size feet I am. I am a size 11, she is a 5. I am 29 years old, she is 23. She likes tea but can't drink coffee. She doesn't like football but likes men who like football. She hates bad spelling, social networking, selfies and all board-games with the exception of chess which she claims to have been playing since she could sit up. It's her birthday soon and I'm invited to her party. I have even made her a present. In summer we're going to Brighton but she'll never let me take her to Blackpool. She says her clothes smell of lavender due to her fabric softener. I tell her mine smell of fried chicken due to the chicken shop below my flat. She doesn't like fried chicken so I promise her that when she comes to stay over I'll be sure to have plenty of lavender air-freshener at hand. Her guilty pleasure is bad music and mine is bad television. She is beautiful and I have a beard.

We've already accepted we're in love. We're going to get married and we're going to have lots of children. I want to get married on a beach, just the two of us but Emilia Rose Parker says "no". She wants a huge family wedding in the church near to where she grew up. I tell her that instead of a three-tiered wedding cake we should have a three-tiered chicken and bacon pie. She surprises me by saying "yes".

If Emilia Rose Parker were a sound then she would be George Harrison's guitar solo in 'Happiness is a Warm Gun'. If she were put in front of your eyes then you would be staring at the sun.

Waiting to meet her has become my whole life. Sometimes I attempt to think her into existence. On days when she doesn't answer her phone I try to communicate with her telepathically or I close my eyes and imagine her standing in front of me. I do this until the image is burnt into my retinas, hoping with all my heart that when I open my eyes she'll be there, tangible and magnificent, beautiful and real.

"I'm going to make it worth your while, it's all I want, all I can think about. We have forever. I just need to sort some things out."

Apparently her friends think that I'm a sexual deviant who'll say anything in order to fulfil my lustful intentions. My friends just assume that she isn't real and tell me to forget about her and move on. I don't care what anybody says or thinks. I can see her in my room. I walk hand in hand with her everywhere I go. In my dreams we've watched many films together, we've showered together, I've stroked her hair when she was ill and I've even played songs to her on my guitar. It won't be long until she materialises and all of this can become reality. No stone unturned, no lavender airfreshener left un-sprayed.

Emilia Rose Parker, a voice at the end of the line. A tome of text messages and a compendium of incredibly beautiful photographs on the screen of my phone. Neither of us have slept properly for days. She says I'm like caffeine, I say she's like cocaine. I don't even remember giving her my phone number but for the past month we've spoken every day for hours at a time.

We talk about everything. Today we've been talking about my ongoing attempts to get published and about her job as a buyer for a new upcoming fashion label I can never remember the name of. Other subjects included: i) her brand new mauve Persian rug, ii) my brand new mauve Primark socks, iii) childhood holidays in Italy, iv) childhood holidays in Skegness, v) her ability to eat a full packet of biscuits in one sitting and still retain her figure, vi) my ability to eat a full packet of biscuits in one sitting and not retain mine, vii) her unused coffee machine, viii) my unpaid bills.

Sometimes Emilia Rose Parker sends me dirty photographs and sometimes she sends me photographs of her breakfast. Sometimes she'll send me a picture of her new dress or her new shoes. I love them all equally.

"I'm going to make it worth your while. It's all I want, all I can think about."

Emilia Rose Parker is always on top form but I'm no slouch.

"What are you doing?" she asks.

"Lying on my bed, staring at the ceiling, playing my guitar."

"Why are you so sexy?"

"Because I only know two chords."

That night I curl up into a ball on my bed and transform into the Colorado River Toad. I find myself somewhere between dreams, smoking a badly rolled cigarette and scratching around on my lily-pad. The waters are murky, the moon is bright. I can hear a family of insects whistling sweet lullabies in the rushes. An ocean wave of distant traffic comforts me.

My psychedelic skin glimmers in the neon lights from the takeaways over the road. I sweat hallucinogens for her and only her. They pulse out of my pores with each tiny beat of my toad heart and roll down my dark green skin like butter in the sun.

I take a long drag of my cigarette and exhale smoke towards the stars, the rushes, the tar black water and the neon lit takeaways. There's a ladybird on the lily-pad opposite me. She notices my cigarette and gives me a disapproving tut. Her burnished shell catches the night sky and casts undulating moonbeams across the water. Wondrous night, phantasmic toad, beautiful ladybird, forgotten human form. A cool damp breeze embraces the cigarette smoke before sending it moonwards, up and up, out of time and out of space.

At the water edge a shadow paces impatiently. Two black marble eyes stare at me. Cold eyes piercing the skin and sending ripples deep into the pond. The ripples reverberate through my lily-pad, into my webbed feet and then into my hollow bones. The ladybird feels the ripples too. She flies towards me and whispers a sweet delicate goodbye in my ear before taking off into the night sky. My mouth lollops in fear; my cigarette falls soundlessly into the water.

I wake up from the dream damp with sweat. I almost managed two hours sleep. This is quite an achievement. I check my phone. Four text messages and one missed call. It's 3:45am. I call Emilia Rose Parker and she answers at the first ring.

"I can't sleep."

"Neither can I."

"Do you know what I'd be if I were an animal yet?"

"I'm working on it."

Part II

A week later she says the hallowed words "Everything is sorted, when do you want to meet?" My heart is an over inflated balloon, my head is television static and my knees are threads. We arrange to meet on the Sunday. She says we should go for a roast dinner, her treat, but I tell her I'd just like to have a drink. I'm sure I'll be far too nervous to eat anything. 2:00pm is the time, location TBC.

Beautiful Parker

Beautiful Sunday

Beautiful Rose

Beautiful 2:00pm

Beautiful Emilia

By Saturday the whole world has ground to a halt. Time teeters forwards and thinks about going backwards. I try to occupy my mind with bad television and loud music. I'm a ten-year-old on Christmas Eve impatiently waiting for Batman figures and Star Wars vehicles. Emilia Rose Parker is almost real. I can feel her somewhere out there in her one-bedroom flat in West Hampstead. I hope that she sleeps tonight. I text her to tell her I'm excited and she texts back immediately with kisses and compliments. She says she'll call me early tomorrow morning and that she can't wait to finally meet me. The weight of it all nearly crushes my spine. I go to bed at 9:30pm equipped with marijuana and whiskey.

I wake up early with a heavy head and a knotted stomach. Excitedly I check my phone but she's not there. No missed calls in the night, no silly text messages, not even a photograph of her breakfast to savour. I try to call but there's no answer. Maybe she's still sleeping?

Emilia Rose Parker, divine mystery, my monstrous lack of sleep, my poetry, my tension headache. Every word she's ever spoken to me suddenly begins to calcify in the back of my head.

"It's all I want, all I can think about."

Sunday is spent mostly in bed throwing text messages into the cosmos and desperately trying to think of excuses for her. Maybe she's hungover, maybe she had to work, maybe she's lost her phone. I imagine it'll be down the back of her settee. I'm sure she'll be in touch.

"The mobile phone you have called is currently unavailable."

Everything is unavailable. I try telepathy but the signal is too faint. I walk to the shop and try to think of anything but her. It's impossible, her image is there with me when I buy biscuits and once more when I see her favourite chocolate bar on offer at two for a pound.

In record time the day is gone. The sun has disappeared and the moon is taunting me at the window. I go to bed, there's little else to do. A shred of hope flickers timidly inside until a light breeze almost, but not quite, extinguishes it completely.

In the dead of night, I stare into the cold heartless soul of my ceiling. The chicken shop extractor fan whirs endlessly until it harmonises with my thoughts. I succumb to madness and allow rejection to swarm over me and take me apart piece by piece. I am almost entirely consumed when the sacrifice is interrupted by the beeping of my phone. One new message, Emilia Rose Parker.

'I am so sorry xxx'

Without hesitation I call her but my number has already been blocked. No explanation... Nothing... Silence... The motion is lost, the mauve Persian rug pulled from underneath my feet, the flame finally extinguished. No more photos of cake, lobster or champagne. No more stories about her small minded grandparents or her big bellied uncle.

No more three tiered chicken and bacon pie. No more calls in the night, drunken text messages or photos of her naked in the bath. No more Emilia Rose Parker.

Part III

Her voice still echoes around my head like an old ghost. All I have for my troubles is a twenty-a-day smoking habit, insomnia and a tension headache. Occasionally I try to convince myself that it was all worth it. That somehow it made me a better person. Her "love yous" made me hallucinate. Every time my shoes let in the rain I think of her.

Emilia Rose Parker, if you read this then you should know that if you were an animal then you would be a racoon.

"The Racoon (Procyon lotor) has learned to wait at the waters edge before pulling a Colorado River Toad away from a lily pad by the back legs, turn it on its back and start feeding on its belly whilst the toad is still alive, a strategy that keeps the racoon well away from the Colorado River Toad's psychoactive poison glands."

"We have forever."

About the Team

Kelcy Boles

Kelcy is an Irish-American bibliophile who really wants to be a citizen of the world. She is currently interning with Jacq Burns, author of *How to Write a Bestseller,* and searching for a way to combine her intense love of all things books and desire to see the world.

Twitter: @kelcy_boles

Saliym Cooper

Saliym always seem to enjoy songs that have the word "fall" in the title. He is currently working on a collection of flash-fiction and a business plan for his future book and record shop.

Twitter: @booksyecouldbe
Website: bookskanyecouldbereading.com/wp

Oisin Harris

Oisin is an itinerant reader who attempts poetry. His work has appeared in Ariadne's Thread, 'The Best Book in the Uni Verse" (PeoplePowerPublications) and Sussex University's newspaper "The Badger". Presently on the MA in Publishing at Kingston University, he hopes to learn how to best combine his love of innovative and engaging literature with the editorial savviness required to help talented writers blossom.

Email: oisin_harris@hotmail.co.uk

Ciara Higgins

Ciara is a book fanatic and a dog lover, and spends her time reading and wishing she had a dog. Her pet project (no pun intended) is a Science-Fiction and Fantasy themed e-magazine featuring predominantly Irish authors, called Animus magazine.

Twitter: @Ciara_Higgins1
Website: animusmagazine.com

Fayola Nivet

Fayola has a lot of feelings about Sci-fi and Fantasy novels that heavily feature relationships between female characters. She's currently in the process of re-writing her novel which flips the script on the portrayal of black and brown people in Portal Fantasy fiction.

Twitter: @fayolazahra
Website: fayolazahra.wordpress.com

Laura Kenwright

Laura read English at Cardiff and then completed an MA in Writing for Stage and Broadcast Media at the Central School of Speech & Drama in London. Outside of her role at Spread the Word, Laura is currently playing around a new writing project involving bringing Arthurian legends to a modern setting, a project which may or may not see the light of day.

Twitter: @lol_valentine

Lightning Source UK Ltd.
Milton Keynes UK
UKOW05f0611280517
302134UK00005B/25/P